Headin' Home to Hell

A Southern Story

By

Richard Goodwyn

Order this book online at www.trafford.com/07-2516
or email orders@trafford.com

Most Trafford titles are also available at major online book retailers.

1. Southern Traditions —Fiction 2. Alabama (State)—
Fiction 3. GLTG—Fiction 4. Lifestyles—Fiction 5. Family Saga—Fiction

This is a work of fiction. Names, characters, places and incidents are either the product of the author's imagination or a composit of typical Southern characteristics. Any resemblance to actual persons, living or dead, events, or locales is entirely coincidental.

Edited by Barbara Heimburger

Note for Librarians: A cataloguing record for this book is available from Library and Archives Canada at www.collectionscanada.ca/amicus/index-e.html

ISBN: 978-1-4251-5616-9

www.trafford.com

North America & international
toll-free: 1 888 232 4444 (USA & Canada)
phone: 250 383 6864 ♦ fax: 250 383 6804
email: info@trafford.com

The United Kingdom & Europe
phone: +44 (0)1865 722 113 ♦ local rate: 0845 230 9601
facsimile: +44 (0)1865 722 868 ♦ email: info.uk@trafford.com

10 9 8 7 6 5 4

For Jim

Thank you for forty-five wonderful years.

ACKNOWLEDGEMENTS

Barbara Heimburger's editing, encouragement and ideas were absolutely crucial to my finished product. Her sense of humor and constant supporting smiles kept me sane. Tod Goldberg's advice was monumental. Finally, Elayne Lewin, Jack Blackburn and Michael J. Lambert read the proof copy when I could no longer read it again without my eyes glazing over. Their contributions were like their friendship, invaluable

I spent the first twenty-nine years of my life in Alabama, my birth state. After thirty years teaching and working in Atlanta, I moved to Palm Springs in 1999 where I now teach part time.

My life and experiences in the South were both rewarding and enlightening. I fondly remember my many friends and family. But they shouldn't look for themselves as a character in this tale; even the town of Kellersville is a product of my imagination.

Prologue

The Queen Bee

Clara Bow Wolfe (named in honor of the American idol of silent-screen era) was born in a rural community outside of Kellersville, a wannabe one-horse town northeast of Montgomery, the state capitol of Alabama. The second and, for medical reasons, the last child of an aging farm couple, she was spoiled beyond rotten. Nothing was denied the darling of Dawson's Ditch, the crossroads where her childhood unfolded. Almost daily trips to Kellersville, Wedowee, and even Alexander City, the closest town of any size, were not drawbacks to the requisite dancing and voice lessons of a future star of stage and screen. In addition, frequent visits to the local department and dress stores were a part of their normal routine. Ma Wolfe had a definite flair for drawing, and because she was also an excellent seamstress, the latest fashion was just a matter of a simple sketch and a good piece of material. Clara Wolfe, an honor graduate of Miss Minnie Mae Prescott's School of Gracious Living, was the best-dressed, most talented and most egotistical girl in her school. Of all the boys from miles around, she could have had her pick, but Clara didn't want to spend the rest of her life picking, boys or anything else, in the country.

After graduation from the county high school, Clara longed for brighter lights. She, like every female, had read *Gone With the Wind* and was convinced her fortune and fame also lay in the city along Peachtree Ridge. Whether she convinced or cajoled her parents into financing the trip to look for a job, she set off to Atlanta in search of a life as far from Dawson's Ditch and Kellersville as possible.

Although she promised them faithfully to return if unsuccessful after a month, she vowed never to return to Kellersville until she could afford to thumb her nose at the pedestrians as she drove down Main Street in a Cadillac.

Her life was going to change and she might as well start with her name. She picked Clairisse; it sounded so French especially since she insisted on using the French spelling and pronouncing it **Claire**-eesse.

After almost a day's ride on the Trailways bus, she arrived in the big city. She had written the Atlanta Chamber of Commerce for information about appropriate residences for professional young ladies and had picked Wesley Arms on West Peachtree Street, despite its suspiciously Methodist-sounding name. It was perfectly located near the center of town and conveniently on the main bus line.

Within the week, she found a waitress job at Mary Mac's Tearoom, a well-known eatery one-block south of the Fox Theatre. Her tenure there was short but productive. She earned enough money to enroll in The Atlanta School of Modeling. When the receptionist's job for the school opened, she pushed her way into the job and worked there for the rest of her year-long quest to be a runway queen. As a result of student modeling jobs, she got some great experience with high-end women's apparel and cosmetics. She made some important contacts in the business, one of whom was Clyde Hopkins, a regional representative for several mid-range labels.

Following a short courtship and a long absence of her period, they were married and moved to Montgomery. Clyde, who lost his job because of poor sales performance, went to work managing the drugstore where his widowed father was the pharmacist. Clairisse used her expertise behind the cosmetic counter until her second pregnancy forced her to quit.

Everything was going at a slow but steady pace until one Saturday night about two months after the birth of Jerry, their second child. Clyde and his father were killed in a head-on-collision on the Tyler Goodwyn Bridge on their way to a bumper sticker appreciation barbecue in Millbrook for the supporters of a local official in the last election.

Left with no one to help with the two babies, no husband, no job, and worse still, no prospects, Clairisse did the only sensible thing. She took some of the insurance money, bought a used Cadillac, and went back to Kellersville.

Within two years, Clairisse had landed the most eligible bachelor in town, Clarence Mitchell. A new resident of Kellersville, Clarence had purchased the ambulance company, the main flower shop and the only funeral home within forty miles. Clairisse got a new Cadillac for her wedding present. The only downside to her success was having to return to Kellersville where, much to her disgust, she was still considered "that girl from Dawson's Ditch."

Charlene Hopkins, Clairisse's first born was unlucky in love—well maybe not in love, but definitely in marriage. Her first two husbands either drank or doped themselves into oblivion. In both cases, Clairisse came into her element and orchestrated the divorce and speedy departure from Kellersville of her former sons-in-law. Charlene dealt with her depressed state by becoming the party-girl of East Alabama.

The closest "Charl," as she had been known during her frolicking years, had ever been to Jesus was the nice Mexican who would occasionally buy her a few belts at the regular Saturday-night beer bash over at the Hog's Trough. But she had to "find The Lord" when Clairisse suddenly decided Charlene should marry the new local Southern Baptist preacher only shortly after his arrival in Kellersville.

Given that Clairisse's second husband was at the doors of the First Holy Free-Will Baptist Church every time they opened, they had become very influential in the congregation. A split in the congregation had come about on an eventful Sunday morning several years before when the preacher stood in the pulpit and shouted "This is God's house and He doesn't want any false idols here. All you women who worship carnal beauty and tarnish His handiwork by painting your faces and frizzing your hair **cannot** and **will not** defile His holy temple and enter unto these premises." Flaying his arms in gigantic circles he screamed "In the name of God Almighty, bar the doors to any wench wearing Satan's war paint."

This serious breech in tenets caused the "painted hussies" to find another house of worship. Charlene, the least of whose sins was a little rouge, and her family moved with the Merle Norman set. The site for the new Second Savior's Holy Free-Will Calvary Baptist Church was just across town.

While the new church was being built, the newly formed congregation held Sunday services in the chapel of the local funeral home, the establishment run by Clairisse's second husband, coincidentally the land donor for the new church building.

Enter George P. Howell, a recent graduate of Delta Junior Technical School in Jackson, Mississippi. He "heard the call" and began to preach at circuit tent revivals throughout rural Mississippi. An influential and well-heeled resident of Kellersville (one of Merle's girls) visited a friend in Alabama's neighboring state and attended one of the revivals where George was preaching. She was so impressed with his sermons and good looks that shortly afterward when the princesses of paint and powder relocated, she convinced the newly-formed Board of Deacons to call George to preach in the recently established Second Free-Will Baptist Church, financed in part by the aforementioned mainstay of the congregation and the town's own Clairisse Wolfe Hopkins Mitchell.

When the new preacher arrived in town, Clairisse went into action. "Charlene, at your age, your options are getting thinner than your brother's hair. This new preacher is an eligible bachelor and he has no idea about your recent life as honky-tonk queen. We need to strike before he gets wind of anything. We have to move fast because there'll be a lot of competition. I've just got to figure out how to defang the local tongues until we can get you married off."

"I don't know if I'm really ready for marrying again. And besides, I don't really care much for this new preacher."

"Nobody said you have to like him, for God's sake. You don't have many opportunities left given your age and, shall I say, experience. Looking around Kellersville at the other old maids, you're like the Hudson on the back of a used car lot, lots of mileage and out of style."

"Thank you Mother. You're one of my greatest admirers. I don't know what I'd do without you around to point out my short-comings."

"Sweetie, folks would see your faults without me. This is Kellersville. Everybody already knows everything about you, most of the men from personal experience."

"I'm for sure not a good candidate for a preacher's wife. Everybody'll laugh their head off at the thought of me living in the door of the church. Besides, I don't have any interest in church. I don't know anything about any of that crap."

"You'll learn. I'll take care of getting you married. The rest is up to you. So find yourself a Bible and get some religion."

The first Sunday's church service would have appeared embarrassingly quick for even a desperate small-town two-time divorcée. So the second Sunday night's prayer service is designated as "D Day."

At the end of the service, Charlene marched right down the aisle during the "call," an indispensable part of any good Sunday-evening or revival preaching which allows the members of the congregation to "rededicate" their life to Jesus and Christian values. Accompanied by the flock's inevitable whining strains of *Just as I Am,* she sank to her knees and loudly proclaimed "Lord, you know I'm a sinner. I want to change my life and be saved. I know I can be a better person and live my life to work in Your service."

There were several pronouncements of "Praise Jesus" and "Amen" from various worshippers.

Then, following Clairisse's carefully written script, Charlene turned toward the congregation and played her trump card. "I beg you all to pray to God to show me the way to redemption so I can be born again in the arms of the Lord."

Marlene McConnell turned to her mother and blurted out just softly enough to give the appearance of trying to be unobtrusive and yet loud enough to be heard for four or five rows in each direction, "Now I've heard it all! She's slept with everyone else in the county. I guess the Lord's the only one left." Horace Tittle was so astonished he dropped the collection plate in Alice Parson's lap which startled her and caused her to jump up with a loud shriek as the coins spilled and rolled down the aisle toward the kneeling group of "saved" souls. Two ten-year-old boys took advantage of the commotion and started grabbing the coins and stuffing them in their pockets.

All in all, it was certainly not the drama Clairisse and Charlene expected. However, Clarisse was banking on the common knowledge that fundamentalists, especially the provincial, small-town variety, are by nature desperate suckers for a good story of repentance and salvation. She was certain they would have Charlene crowned and enshrined by the first hair appointment on the following Tuesday morning. A good soul cleansing had always been a catharsis, especially if "witnessed."

Because Clairisse's second husband left her the family businesses, the local funeral parlor and adjoining cemetery, she was generally regarded a woman of moderate means (some of which financed the church) and in a fairly influential position in the community. For these reasons, her daughter was considered a good catch regardless of two divorces and numerous past transgressions. And after all, she had been "saved" and born again. It wasn't long until, with a great deal of the manipulation that made Clairisse so formidable, the parsonage had a new mistress.

Now after having taken a quick refresher course from a renowned teaching source: "Drive Yourself to Heaven in Twelve Complete Taped Lessons" ($19.95 + S&H, free Bible included: red-letter edition $1.00 extra), Charlene was teaching Sunday school and her Ladies Auxiliary Society was the most active in this area of the state.

Part I

Thomas Wolfe was right when he wrote
"You can't go home again."
But sometimes, there is no choice!

One

Just When You Think...

Of all the plans for my life in California, none of them included returning to Alabama for more than the two-day hops at the first and last of August to pick up PK for our annual father-son month together. There was a time I called Kellersville home. Now, 'home' is the last word that comes to mind when I think of that little town in the east-central part of the state.

Once, while I was still living in New York, Nan brought PK to Montgomery because I had booked turn-around tickets to avoid spending even one night in the "Heart of Dixie." This time, however, I have a ticket to Atlanta with an open return. Every time I buy a ticket to Atlanta, I think of the popular saying "To go to hell from anywhere in the South, you have to first change planes in Atlanta." That is exactly where I'm going—straight to hell, by way of Atlanta of course!

The phone startles me out of my rambling thoughts. As I glance at the screen on the receiver, I recognize the number on the caller ID.

"Luke, I called you hours ago. Where the hell have you been?" I blurt out as I pick up the receiver.

"Ah've been in At-lannah at thuh bar-be-cue wif ahall thuh othur belles."

Even without modern-day technology, there is no mistaking the voice on the other end of the line. The heavy fake Southern accent does not disguise the voice of my agent, Luke Styles.

"Hawaper, Iah jus got yo fon message sayin' yore goin' back to wher…**evah** the hay-ull it was that you uu-esed to live, pah-don me, egg-**zist**! Ha-ave you lawst yo my-yend?"

"Luke, give it a rest! Even Scarlet O'Hara couldn't understand you."

"Aw honey, you'd take the fun out of a wet dream."

"I was just putting the last few things in the bags. If you had waited another ten minutes, I'd have been on the way to the airport."

"I'm surprised you haven't already been carried away by the loony police," Luke retorts in his normal voice, just as exaggerated but without the hog jowl. "And that won't be pretty, honey. Those straight jackets are really a misnomer and totally impossible to accessorize."

"Luke, I'm not moving there. It's just an extended visit. Can you interrupt your pilgrimage to Tara long enough to meet me at the Atlanta airport so I can fill you in on all the details?"

"How about in front of the baggage claim? I'll be the one in the hoop skirt." He hangs up quickly to avoid any further opportunity for me to protest any possibility of public embarrassment.

As I put down the receiver, I can't keep the doubts and fears from rushing back into my head more puzzling than before. I immediately feel guilty because of this momentary flash of apprehension about my decision to return to the place of my youth for such a long period of time, even under the dire circumstances. Then I ask myself why I even hesitate; it's a no-brainer!

Two

Doing What Comes Naturally

During the six-hour flight to Atlanta, I have a seat next to the window. Since the aisle seat is unoccupied, I have an opportunity to reminisce about my youth in Kellersville. Nan and I were the proverbial childhood sweethearts. No one ever considered we weren't an item. Nan moved to Kellersville with her mother when she was two years old. I was a third-generation native, an aristocrat by Kellersville standards. Nan was the ever bubbly and popular cheerleader as well as the president of her class all four years. I was quieter and more studious. I didn't get interested in school politics until my senior year when I ran for president of the Student Government Association and won. We were very involved in most of the same extracurricular clubs and organizations so we were together constantly. When we went off together to the University of Alabama, it seemed to be the natural order of things.

After finishing our studies at the university, we returned to Kellersville and took jobs teaching at the same school where we had spent our high-school years.

I replaced William Porter Warren. Kellersville's legendary English teacher also sponsored the *Huntsman* which had once won recognition in a state yearbook contest. Mr. Warren's reputation as an eccentric was born in the late seventies when he began requiring every student in the class to complete a needle-point project representing a significant scene from one of the novels on the reading list for that year. The occasional visitor to his classes was flabbergasted by the sight of senior football players doing the basket weave or embroidery while listening to another student reading poetry or a passage from the current literary selection. My project garnered special praise and was still hanging in Mr. Warren's classroom on the "wall of honor" amid the four other all-time winners when I went to interview for the position to replace the seemingly larger-than-life paragon of literary prowess. Mr. Warren had generously offered to leave his "trophies" and the detailed instructions for the project so I could carry on the tradition. He actually appeared genuinely dismayed when I insisted he take the collection home for enjoyment during his retirement years.

Nan's specialty was American History. She made the story of our country come alive for her students. She loved teaching the Civil War. Her organization of a reenactment for Kellersville High School really motivated even the most disinterested students. Her efforts were always applauded by her peers and the community. The real validation came when she was selected Teacher of the Year for the state of Alabama. That year the event had been filmed and appeared frequently on the statewide educational television network. She organized a Kellersville High Academy Awards presentation and the entire school voted on the winners. Nan was a professional and personal triumph; everybody adored her.

Our marriage fifteen years ago was a foregone conclusion for everyone, especially the two of us. Getting married and raising a family was the expected way of life in a small-town Southern rural environment and Kellersville was no different. No one ever did anything else. Few ambitions included living outside the comfort afforded by family and friends and certainly nobody ever left by choice; one was eternally a product and possession of Kellersville. Although Nan and I definitely had more exposure to the outside world because of our years at the university, we had spent our entire lives in preparation to follow the prescription for happiness. Even then, however, I suspected fate was throwing me a curve. I know now I took the path of least resistance although in the depths of my gut I feared it was a dead-end street.

When PK arrived the next year, I knew my life had radically changed forever. I could see myself settling down in Kellersville and retiring as the old eccentric small-town English teacher. In my nightmares, I envisioned myself in a classroom surrounded by students bound head to toe in knitting yarn with needles and pins sticking out all over their bodies. I often woke up in a sweat and with a dry mouth, convinced it was a prophetic vision of my future.

And then the most bizarre and inexplicable thing happened. Almost over night my first novel was an immediate and gigantic success! Luke Styles, my agent, had recognized my enormous talent and organized the public relations campaign of every author's dreams.

Five years ago, I left Kellersville on a promotional tour for the book. Nan and I told family and friends that as soon as the tour was over and I had found a suitable apartment for the three of us, Nan and PK would join me in New York. Neither of us thought it would be so easy to disguise the real reason for the separation. Since the tour was to last almost a year, it would give us time to make a more suitable explanation for my moving to New York alone.

Nan had been the first to broach the subject. She said she spent many months trying to ignore the evident signs: moodiness, pensiveness, secret phone calls, and longer than normal workout sessions at the gym in the neighboring town. I don't think I was that obvious, by either physical appearance or actions, but she noticed I did react differently when certain attractive men were around. All together, these pieces fit into the situation Nan had suspected since high school; I was attracted to other men.

One evening after a very pleasant dinner with John and Harriet Thompson, who worked at the same school, Nan asked in a quiet inquiring tone.

"Do you think Harriet is aware you and John are having an affair?"

It was just that quick! To the point and calculated to preempt a planned response.

I take a deep breath and reply, "I was wondering how long it would be before we had this conversation. How long have you known?"

"About your tendencies or your affair with John?"

"Both, actually."

"I guess I first noticed something different about you in high school, but I wasn't sure what it was. Later in college, I began to notice the way you perked up around certain guys, especially the ones I thought were cute like Tommy Knox."

"Yeah, he did get my attention, but that's all."

"I really had nothing concrete to base my opinion on, just feelings. I suppose I went through the normal doubts. Was it me? Was I not attractive enough? Had you grown tired of me? Had I done something to cause us to grow apart physically?"

"Of course not! Don't be foolish! None of this is your fault!"

"Oh I know that *now*, but *then* was another story. When we got married, I thought everything was going to change and for a while, I thought it had. We were so happy after PK came. Then I noticed things going back to the way they were before."

"I didn't realize I was so transparent."

"Not to everyone else. But don't forget, I've known and loved you since kindergarten. I noticed every time you lost a hair."

I caught myself unconsciously raising my right hand to the lion's pride, the lusciously thick mane which framed my still boyish face.

"As far as you and John are concerned, I really had nothing concrete until last summer when we all rented that cabin in the mountains. It seemed you and John invented reasons to be alone. Fishing? Harper, really! The only thing you ever fished for was a compliment."

"Do you think Harriett knows?" I ask expecting to validate my opinion that she didn't have a clue about anything unrelated to Home Economics.

Harriet Thompson had spent the better part of her life, both professional and personal, preparing herself to be the effervescent June Cleaver of Kellersville, the perfect wife and mother who habitually ignored unpleasant things such as reality. Her motto was, "If it's not pretty, don't look at it." This scenario had no place in the chapter on the all-around American family.

"I've not seen any indication of it. You know she's not the sharpest knife in the drawer. I'm not sure she would believe it if she found out. Besides, how could she? This subject is not covered in any Home Economics book I've ever seen."

At that point, I take a deep breath and place my neck on the altar. "My relationship with John isn't the real point of this conversation, is it?

"No. We've got things to discuss and decisions to make. You love me too much to leave me, and I love you too much to hold you here. And there's PK to consider. If anything ever happened…"

"Nothing will ever happen. I would never do anything to embarrass you or PK."

"I know that, but people talk. In a small town, even the most insidious idle gossip soon becomes fact. Kellersville is a fertile breeding ground for *tittle tattle* as it is. Even the most righteous would have a field day with something like this. The fear of the unknown and misunderstood is always a threat. Your career is also a concern. Even though you may never want to teach again, there would always be a skeleton in your closet if it became a part of your permanent file."

"You're right. I'm so sorry it's come to this. I love you and I would never do anything to hurt you."

"You could never hurt me except by hurting yourself or PK. But it's time for you to live a real life."

Three

A New Beginning: An Old Story

There was no denying it; my life had made a complete u-turn. I went from a small-hick-town English teacher to a best-selling author of four novels, the last of which had just been released.

Shortly after I bought my house in Southern California, a reporter from the local magazine *Palm Springs Life* called to interview me for a cover story.

As she took a seat in the booth opposite my seat, her opening words made an immediate connection.

"My name is Samantha Harrell, but you can just call me Sammie. If you think this drawl is put on for your benefit, I've got to own up. I'm straight out of the Delta dirt of Mississippi. I picked *A Bit of Country* for us to meet 'cause they have grits just like momma used to make."

"I love grits. I'm glad to know they have them here." I could feel myself immediately slipping back into my Southern persona. "The French have their bread, the Italians their pasta, the Mexicans their tortillas, and we Southerners have our grits."

"And of course, nobody cares what the Yankees eat."

"Where in Mississippi?

"You've never heard of it, honey. A little town near Greenville named Itta Bena."

"The hell I haven't. My roommate for four years at the University of Alabama was Harry Dennis!"

"Oh my God! He married my sister!"

"Helen's your sister? I was best man at their wedding! But I don't recognize you."

"I wouldn't expect you to. At the time, I was fourteen, wore pigtails, had a huge set of braces and there was more meat on a rack of spareribs than on my entire body. Since then of course, I've porked up, lost the braces, cut my hair and grown tits."

I couldn't stop myself. I cackle out loud. I love her already! "Jesus, that makes me feel old. I haven't heard from them for over five years. How are they? Is Harry still practicing law with your daddy?

"When it's not hunting season. Of course in the South, there's always something to hunt. If they're not hunting, they're getting ready for it or getting over it. God, I can't imagine anything more boring. And it's terribly unnecessary! And what's so awful about going to the *Winn Dixie*? By the time you pay for all the gear, it's cheaper and certainly a lot less trouble."

"Did you go to The University?"

"Alabama? Lord no, honey. I'm Ole Miss, magnolias and all. 'Once you've tried the rest, Tri Delt, we're the best.'"

"How did you end up in Palm Springs?"

"I'm supposed to be asking you that question. How did you wind up here?"

"When I left Alabama, I moved to New York. At first, I was enthralled with the shows, restaurants and social life. But it was too frantic for a small-town Alabama boy. My next choice was, of course, San Francisco. I soon realized I couldn't live there. After so many years in the closet, I was too easily sidetracked from my work by the party atmosphere. I never got anything done."

"I know what you mean. I tried it for a short time. There was just too much temptation, even for a party girl from Ole Miss."

"And then there was the health crisis. I was scared beyond reason. Of course, LA was out of the question for all the same reasons and a dozen more. Besides, people are trying to get *out* of LA, not *in*. While I was in the Bay Area, I made several trips to the desert with friends. I loved it here. There's a small-village atmosphere with a cosmopolitan attitude and a dream climate, except of course July and August. As soon as I got back to the Bay Area, I started making arrangements to move."

"I read *Of Many Chances, None Remain* and loved it. How did you get the idea for such an unusual murder mystery? Is *Portmanville* modeled on your hometown, Kellersville?"

"Well, yes and no. It's a typical small Southern town."

"How about the characters? Are they people you know?"

"All characters are fictional. That's my story and I'm sticking to it."

The rest of the interview was very pleasant and passed much more quickly than I realized. We parted after agreeing to meet sometime for a cocktail and more down-home talk.

When I really think about it, I've settled easily into the Old Movie Colony, the section of town where the original bungalows of the stars are located from the Thirties and Forties. My typical day follows a comfortable and somewhat flexible pattern consisting of a light breakfast, crossword puzzle, gym, lunch and an afternoon-long work session occasionally capped off by dinner with friends.

I love to cook for relaxation. Watching the evening news while preparing supper [For me, it will always be supper; the common name for the evening meal in the South.] gives me an opportunity to gear down for a quiet pleasure-reading session before retiring early.

I rarely go out except on the weekends. Even though California's smoking laws have thankfully changed the air quality, nothing has happened to alter the cat-n-mouse games which are the mainstay of bars everywhere; meaningful and interesting conversational topics are mutually exclusive of physical attractiveness. In fact, when on the rare occasion I find both attributes in the same person, the guy is generally already partnered.

I'm not eaten up by ego, but I do consider myself a nicely-built thirty-nine-year-old with graying-blonde hair who is trying to move gracefully into middle age. I take care of my skin and thanks to consistent and persistent care it remains nearly flawless, especially for my age and fair skin tone, which is a minor miracle in the desert sun. Of course, I constantly work on my body, not so much for appearance sake, while certainly not unimportant, but for the health benefits; both of my parents experienced heart disease.

All in all, for whatever reason, it seems I've managed to gather my own line of admirers, none of whom meet the "interesting conversationalist" standard on my evaluation scale. The idea that disturbs me the most is, although I am fortunately on *their* lists for a good romp, it is always with a minimal exchange of dialogue. I feel as though no one likes me for more than the few hours it takes for a couple of drinks and a quick roll in the sack; if dinner is included, it's a bonus. The result is I usually have as much sex as I want, but emotional attachment and commitment continue to elude me.

The sad result of all this being Nan is still the only person with whom I have ever established a meaningful relationship. Now, that part of my life is about to come to an end.

Four

Short Time—Long Trip

When I emerge from the seemingly mile-long escalator shaft in the Atlanta airport, my eyes quickly scan the waiting crowd on the left near the baggage claim area and breathe a sigh of relief. No hoopskirt in sight! Luke is infamous for playing his vacation scenarios to the hilt. The castanets are still ringing in my ears from last year's trip to Spain. Luckily, it looks as if Luke has sensed the seriousness of the current situation and has appeared in khaki shorts and a Brooks Brothers cotton shirt, lime sherbet, but still tasteful and within the realm of normal.

"How was the flight?" Luke asks as he hugs me.

"It was uneventful. I got a nap and a chance to work a little. There was no food, not that it would have been edible. I'm starving. As soon as I get the rental car and get out of the airport, we need to find a place to eat and talk."

Baggage claim is the usual zoo. Luke and I spend the twenty-five-minute wait for the bags talking business. Luke expresses concern about meeting upcoming deadlines for the next draft.

"Just thought I'd mention the publishing whores are licking their chops for the outline of number five. How's it going?"

I try to allay his concerns by a response with a casual "Oh it's coming along. Don't worry."

"I didn't say I was worried. I'm just more than a little apprehensive about this vacation in a non-productive environment."

"First of all, it's not a vacation. And have you forgotten that this non-productive environment was the birthplace of Harriet Hawkins, detective extraordinaire?"

"Well, that was then and this is now." Luke obviously can no longer contain his curiosity and asks, "What's going on anyway?"

I don't think the short trip to pick up the Budget Rental car I have reserved is enough time to get into the details. "Let's wait until we get a quieter place to talk."

Luke nods. "Agreed, but let's eat first. I'm starving."

I spy a Waffle House, a ubiquitous short-order has house chain in most states of the Southeast. "How about the Waffle House?"

"You mean the 'Awful House?' Luke moans through his lips which he has contorted in his usual sign of disgust.

" It's probably as good a choice as any since this section of Atlanta doesn't offer a wide array of gourmet restaurants to choose from. Besides, I want to get on the road to Alabama as soon as possible and the convenience to I-85 is a plus."

As we walk in the door, we are greeted by our waitress, Inez [pronounced EYE nez], a dumpy middle-aged tired looking woman in her fifties with "I. L.O.V.E J.E.S.U.S" tattooed on her individual fingers.

"Welcome to the Waffle House honey. Y'all come right on in. There ain't no hostess so y'all just sit anywhere you can find a clean booth."

She walks up holding an order pad, pulls a stubby pencil out of her inky-black home-dyed Church of God hairdo, which frames the typical cardboard headband with the Waffle House logo, touches the lead tip to her tongue and drawls "Hi, hon. What y'all havin' this morning?"

Luke flips the plastic covered menu to the reverse side where the breakfast items are listed. "I'll have coffee, wheat toast, no butter and fresh fruit."

Inez looks up from her order pad and grins. "Hon, the only fruit in this joint ain't in a bowl! Don't get me wrong, my boyfriend, Ray, over there is as gay as Chinese arithmetic and I don't care, but get a grip, this is the Waffle House not the Hilton."

She calls out to the short order cook, a squatty and fairly pudgy man in his early to late fifties standing at the grill. His stringy dark-brown hair emerges from under the army-style paper cap revealing the remnants of a peroxide bottle gone haywire.

"Hey, Rayleene."

"Yeah, honey."

"This guy over here ordered some **fresh fruit**." She can hardly get the elongated words out of her mouth for the laughter.

Ray giggles, turns toward them, puts his hands on his hips which he wiggles in a sexual circular motion and responds toward Luke, "Nez Honey, you come on over here and cook these eggs. I'll be right over and see what I can do to serve up some **fruit**. But I don't know how **fresh** it's gonna be 'cause I ain't been home since last night."

I almost strangle and lose control laughing into my glass of water. "I guess y'all see a lot of gays being in this location and open twenty-four hours."

"Yeah, honey."

A giggly echo rolls in from the cook station: "Yeah, child."

I haven't had grits since the wonderful interview at Bit of Country in Palm Springs. Since I love corn in all fashions and forms, I speak up with a question to which I really already know the answer. "I hope y'all have grits."

Inez grins. "Yeah, honey."

Ray drones from behind her. "Yeah, child."

"I'd like two lightly-scrambled eggs, grits and toast."

"Coffee?"

I chuckle, "Yeah, honey" and glance toward Ray who is busy plating a waffle for the old bag lady at the end of the counter.

"Yeah, child."

"And you sweetie, do you still want some of that fruit?" Inez can hardly contain herself.

"Probably just the toast and coffee will do for now. I'll take a rain check on Ray!"

"We'll get right on it!"

Ray breaks in, "Yeah, honey!"

The three of us respond in unison, "Yeah, child!"

As soon as Inez leaves our booth, I turn toward Luke and finally break the silence about the reason for the sudden decision to return to Kellersville. "Nan is dying."

Luke's face drains of its usual peachiness as he gasps "Oh my god!" He slaps his right palm across his chest to the upper left breast, a dramatic movement to emphasize extreme astonishment, which we call in the South call *broach clutching*. "I had no idea. What's wrong? How long has she been sick? Why haven't you said something before now?"

"In July when I went to pick up PK for our trip to Canada, Nan told me she had been diagnosed with diabetes. They were treating her with insulin and the usual regimen. Not only was she showing no signs of improvement, but she also seemed to be getting worse on a daily basis.

Last week, Hank took her to Birmingham to the University Medical Center because the doctors in Kellersville couldn't get her blood sugar under control. After further tests, they realized the local doctors had screwed up the diagnosis. It's pancreatic cancer. There's nothing they can do. They told her to get her affairs in order as soon as possible. She's got three to five months at the most."

"God Harper, I'm so sorry. You must be devastated. I know you still love her very much. What about PK? How is he taking it?"

"Actually she and Hank are waiting for me to get there to tell him. It's all happening so quickly. School has already started. Hank is tied up every waking minute with the football season so he's between a rock and the proverbial hard spot when it comes to being there during the day. Very soon he won't be able to go off and leave Nan alone while he is working, and they can't afford to hire someone to be there fourteen hours a day. The salary for two teachers in rural Alabama is barely enough to keep them going."

"Aren't you still sending money?"

"Of course I am. When we divorced, I agreed to pay the house off and send money for the utilities along with very ample support for PK. When Hank came on the scene, he didn't want Nan to accept anything but the monthly support for PK."

"Do they have any savings?"

"I don't really know. Hank's grandmother died shortly after they married. He inherited a small amount when she died. I doubt it lasted long."

"What about the insurance? Doesn't it cover the medical bills?"

"Yes, but they pay only eighty percent. And then there's the possibility of home nursing care which is not covered. I offered to pay it directly, but Hank wasn't comfortable accepting the money."

"Is there no family on either side to help?"

"Nan's mother was an orphan. When she died, there was no one left in her family. Her dad had some family somewhere in Arkansas, but we never had any contact with them. And Hank's mother can't help. She remarried a career military man and they're stationed in Japan. When it comes down to it, there is only one solution. Hank has agreed for me to come and help. So I decided to stay here until something happened. Besides, I wanted this last opportunity to be with her."

"He sounds like a real macho dunce! I mean it really doesn't make any sense to refuse monetary support from your wife's ex-husband, but let him live in the house under foot."

"He's actually a very smart guy, a math teacher and *very* hunky. When we were teaching together, I had a crush on him, big time. He's the football coach; a jock and you know how that turns most of us on."

"Oh?" Luke then adds, "I've heard this is a particularly vicious illness."

"It is. The track record for surviving this cancer is the worst, in fact non-existent!"

Inez returns with the food. I avert my eyes to the front door in an effort to avoid looking at her hands when she places the plates in front of us. I have already seen enough to curb my appetite, which under the circumstances is relatively nonexistent.

"If y'all need anything else honey, just holler." She says by rote.

Luke gets into the act. "Yeah, honey"

I laugh for the last time that day. "Yeah, child."

Luke speaks as he is breaking his toast and spreading it with the contents of one of those little yellow and white plastic packets which claim to contain some flavor of jelly. "What about PK? Do you think he can handle having his dad move back under the circumstances?"

"Why do you ask that question?"

"After all, your relationship has been great for one month out of the year, but you haven't spent any time together in Kellersville since he was nine. You've always picked him up and spirited him away on the magic carpet. From what I understand, he really doesn't know you or anything about your personal life. You always went into the closet for your summer trips together. Does he even know you're gay?"

I sense my head lowering as I reply with what is apparently a twinge of doubt in my voice, "I don't know, but at this point, we have no choice. We'll have to do the best with what we have. All I know is Nan seems to be relieved and grateful I'm coming to help."

"Will people talk in that little burg?"

"All that matters is my family. As for everyone else, I've outgrown being a slave to small-town opinion. I'm doing what I have to do. If Nan and Hank can deal with the gossip, I can handle it for the short time I'll be there."

Then Luke drops the bomb. "What will you do with PK when Nan dies?"

"What do you mean? He's my son. He'll go back to California with me." I quickly blurt out. "Do you really think I'd stay in Kellersville? With Nan gone, there's nothing there for me except PK."

"How much do you really know about him? After all, you said yourself you don't see him but an average of once a year."

"Even though I am not still enjoying day-to-day contact with him, I have learned that he's not your typical Southern small-town teenage boy. His acute interest in computers and reading, especially the classics, set him apart from the usual daily activities of his peers."

"Is that good or bad?" interjects Luke.

"Good or bad, it seems natural since he is the progeny of two sensitive, intelligent, education-minded individuals. His home environment has always been different."

"Does he have any close friends?"

"He has a couple of close pals, but most of his friends are the girls who take an interest in cultural pastimes rather than cheerleading, makeup and the usual giggly schoolgirl gossip."

"He's been sort of different since he was a baby, even when it comes to his name. We gave him the name Parker Lee Wolfe and planned to call him Parker. However, he quite innocently created his own nickname. When he was learning to write his name, he began making the P and K disproportionately larger than the other letters resulting in the outstanding PK moniker."

"How old is he now?"

"He was only nine years old when I left Kellersville and I've been gone almost six years."

"So he is full in the middle of the most difficult period of his life, the teens."

"That's true. I'm not fooling myself that it is going to be easy bringing him to live with me. My life is really going to change, again. But I do know more about him than you think. Since he is blessed with my talent as a good writer and is also a faithful correspondent, we keep very close contact. Often times, he reveals facts and feelings he guards at home. Nan tells me that usually, after a couple of days privately reading and rereading each successive e-mail, PK prints it and shares selected parts with her and Hank at the dinner table. Through these weekly e-mails, we plan the upcoming summer's itinerary and activities to the letter. Nan is overjoyed he we are maintaining such close communication. PK does computer research on our projected trip and by the time the departure time arrives, he has every day's activities mapped out. To say he eagerly anticipates our vacations together seems a gross understatement."

"Well, it's still not going to be a walk in the park. As long as you realize it from the beginning!"

"I know it. I've certainly thought a lot about it since I found out about Nan's condition."

What about your family? Don't you still have an aunt there? I thought there were cousins and such."

"Oh! Yeah. After years with a not-so-cheap but effective therapist, I had almost forgotten: dad's sister and her brood."

"Won't they help?"

"I doubt it. Except for Charlene, her daughter, we never got along that well because I refused to bow down to Clairisse's iron-handed control. The only three people she couldn't whip into shape were my father, her second husband and me. Although God only knows she made control a full-time job. I spent my childhood defying her every attempt to run my life. By the time I reached high school, she put me in the category with my father, lost causes. Since her late second husband had a mind of his own, she placed all her energy on everyone else. Her children weren't strong enough to survive and most likely they're still in tow."

"Maybe she's changed. After all, family crises often rally estranged family members."

"Unlikely miracle. The last time I heard from Charlene, she was still the wicked witch of East Alabama. Charlene, Nan and I were very close in high school. I still get cards at Christmas with a line or two. Nothing's changed."

"But you're still part of their family. Maybe they'll be sympathetic and come to your rescue."

"Maybe, but I'm not sure it would be worth the price."

"Do you still have contact with your aunt?"

"Not really. After Mom and Dad died, she hasn't had much to do with me. I can't say I've missed her. I've done everything I could to ignore her. All of them except Charlene have certainly ignored me. I was rarely included in their family functions, not that I would have gone. More to the point, there wasn't room for me at the table with all their ex-spouses and illegitimate yard urchins. Their lives were, and I assume still are, fodder for a soap opera. I could write a best seller about all their lives, but I'm sure they would sue me for slander. I still feel guilty about leaving PK there even with Nan to protect him."

"Will you be staying with Hank and Nan? Do they have room for you?" asks Luke as he picks up the check.

Luke pays at the register and I leave Inez a big tip on the table. As we walk to the parking lot, I finally answer Luke's question.

"Yes, I'm staying with them. They have a third bedroom. It'll be easier when the going gets rough. Here's the phone number and address. You have my cell, but I don't plan to leave it on all the time, only when I leave the house. You'll be able to reach me at their house most of the time."

"Good luck. Keep in touch. If it gets too much for you, you can always come to 'Hotlanta' for the weekend. "Here's John's new number. I'm going back next week, but give John a call in case you need a place to stay. He quit smoking last January and the stench is just about out of the house by now. He would be very happy for you to come. He is very fond of you and would do anything to help especially under the present circumstances."

"I'm not sure I'm willing to pay the rent. A hotel would be cheaper and more restful."

"Well, just keep it in mind."

"Thanks, I will."

"Considering what's ahead for you, I'm not going to push too hard about work. I hope you can find some time to find another murder plot in Kellersville. You might consider your Aunt Clairisse for the deserving victim. She sounds perfect for the role."

"Trust me. I'll keep her in mind. She's always been on my list of possible victims. I guess I haven't done it yet because then all the fun of planning the excruciating pain of her demise would be over."

"Perhaps that's the closure you need."

"Not now. The options are still open. I'm heading home you know."

Luke hugs me and adds, "Call me if there's anything..."

"Thanks."

I start the car and head toward one of the hardest tasks of my life; saying goodbye to the only woman besides my mother I have ever loved.

Five

Some Things Never Change Some Things Change Forever

When I awake the morning after arriving in my beloved Kellersville, I navigate the familiar path from the bathroom to the kitchen to get a cup of that magic potion which will allow my eyes to open and greet the morning. Out of years of sheer habit, I unconsciously reach for the most recent edition of the local weekly from its usual spot on the kitchen table and head toward my favorite morning spot, the glass-enclosed sun porch on the eastern side of the living room. Stepping into the morning light, the sunrise begins to instantly warm the body and spirit. I realize I am at home. I have greeted many sunrises in this spot and the comfortable re-acquaintance with the over-stuffed chair in the corner eases me into a reminiscence of my boyhood and life as a young adult in the town of my origin.

Then suddenly the thought occurs to me that I was never really overly unhappy here; in point of fact, just the *opposite*. Until Nan and I left for the university, I was very satisfied. It wasn't until just recently that I realized one's requirements for happiness could change as they indeed had for me within the past year. Kellersville was and always will be the same. I have become a different person.

My gaze moves up and I spy Myrtle Woods, our next-door neighbor for all my life, working in her dahlia garden as she has done every warm morning for as long as I can remember. When she looks up and casually waves hello, I know my being here is definitely no surprise to her or to anyone else within a twenty-mile radius.

Has it been so long that I could have forgotten the lightening speed with which news travels and the amazing embellishment of the facts as they spread in every direction like an errant drop of mustard to even the most unexpected place on a white shirt? Within the space of one morning, the details of my return has probably provided more interesting information than a month of *The Kellersville Tribune*, last night's eighteen-wheeler collision on the Wedowee Highway, and the farm and livestock report on WKVL, combined.

I can't help but smile as I realize coffee sales will soar out of sight at the the *Koffe Korner*, the lunch counter in Petersons's Pharmacy which Mazie Green has leased and run with her sister, Hazel Hope, for the last thirty-five years. During this time, they have provided coffee and homemade cakes in the mornings, blue-plate specials of locally grown vegetables during the noon hour, and the local hot spot for "inquiring minds" on the town square. All the merchants of the stores, shops and offices that line the perimeter of the central town square are drawn to these daily gatherings like the gaze of the rubbernecks who cannot summon enough control to pass an accident without gawking at the scene, the gorier the better. There is no use going to a store or office before eleven in the morning. The doors open as usual at nine, but everyone starts to congregate at Petersen's by nine-thirty. Failure to make an appearance is dangerous. If the reason someone is missing is unknown to the coffee drinkers, all the better. Speculation is always more entertaining and imaginative than fact.

I also know that by noon of the day after my arrival, the local ladies are busy cooking the requisite pies, cakes and casseroles to take to the Warner home on their mission to gather enough information to make them the center of attention at Belle's Beauty Bar. At Belle's, you are guaranteed a curl: your hair by a cheap perm or your toes by the latest tidbit of homegrown gossip.

Seeing Nan last night was unnerving. Even with all the warning from Hank, I hadn't been prepared for how she looked. I was not expecting her once peaches-and-cream complexion to have the tint of rancid butter. Her sallow eyes had lost their mischievous luster and dimmed the beacons of her effervescence. I quickly tried to recover from the first encounter, but it was evident by her reaction she felt sorry for my evident despair. She knew from many years of dealing with my emotional weakness in these situations I wasn't capable of taking another step at that point. Almost as if on cue, PK came in to save the moment. It was, however, only temporary. We had to deal.

PK is very astute for a fourteen-year-old small-town boy. However, all three of us dread telling him the details of Nan's illness and the prognosis, although as it turns out, his awareness of the illness and its consequences would have surprised all three of us. In spite of having guessed the truth, he breaks down when we finally tell him the details. The main shock for PK is how quickly everything is happening. He really had no idea his mother would die so soon. He struggles to hold back the tears, but they well in his eyes and stream down his cheeks.

He collapses into sobs when Hank hugs him and whispers, "Crying is the way we have to share our emotions with the people we love. All of us are crying together."

No one broaches the subject of future plans, but we are well aware that questions are running through PK's mind. I'm sure there is no way anyone can have the slightest idea about the turmoil that is battering the mental state of this typical teenager. None of the many sleepless nights he spends tossing and turning restlessly in the dark ever produces any answers to the questions that are plaguing his adolescent mind. What will happen when Nan dies? Will I want him? Will he go with me or will I leave him here with Hank? Will he have a choice? If so, what will he do? Kellersville is all he knows. He doesn't know if he will like living in California. It just isn't fair. Moving to another school in a part of the country that is so foreign to him is really scary. He has his friends in Kellersville and he feels comfortable where he is. I am sure he has grown to love and respect Hank, but he isn't his dad. While their relationship has obviously been super, his mother has always been here as a catalyst. How would it be without her? He doesn't even know if Hank wants him to stay. This is all a big part of it. He feels helpless on every side. His mother is dying and his life is falling apart. It's too much for a fourteen-year-old under any circumstances.

No one knows the right thing to say. Finally Nan breaks the long tearful silence. "Honey, we know this is all so hard for you. We all love you and realize you are in for a lot of changes in your life. We'll have a lot to talk about tomorrow, but for now, we just need to love and support each other. Hank has put together a nice supper and we need some time to be together."

"I'm not real hungry right now." This pronouncement underscores PK's apparent anguish. Like every average fourteen-year-old boy, eating is always on his agenda. "Why does it have to be so fast? Can't they give you something? Kathy's mother lived for five years after she got sick. Can't you go to another doctor?"

"Honey, I went to the University Hospital in Birmingham. They all say the same thing. Kathy's mother had a different type of cancer. They could treat her in a different way. The type of cancer I have can't be treated. They've already done all they can do. I know it's going to be hard, but you can help me by keeping your chin up. Let's get the most out of the time we have." PK falls into her arms sobbing.

Six

Family Matters

I knew it was just a question of time before someone from the family showed up to pick for the details of my return. I didn't have long to wait. That afternoon, Charlene, my first cousin, arrived unannounced.

Nobody bothers to call in small Southern towns; dropping by is normal. Calling ahead is reserved for only more formal occasions and certainly not for family, regardless of how estranged or how long it has been. Doors are rarely locked to avoid a contagious curiosity. Why would one lock the door if there were nothing to hide?

"Yoo-hoo! Anybody home?" A whining shriek accompanying a courtesy tapping on the screen door resounds through the house.

I look up and almost stagger backwards. It has to be a time warp! Charlene looks exactly the same as when I last saw her, plain and dumpy. I am convinced she's even wearing the same dress. Although I'm sure she has shampooed her hair at least once during this time, it looks like she must have done so without removing a single pin or disturbing a single wave. Charlene's popularity in school was definitely not based on her looks. She was, however, well known as one of the *friendliest* girls in Kellersville.

I'm jolted back to the present by the shrillness of Charlene's voice as it echoes through the folds of my memory.

"My Gawd, Harper, you haven't changed a bit. Still handsome as ever. Thank goodness you still have your gorgeous wavy hair.

Momma used to say she didn't understand why you got the beautiful hair in the family and I got this thin, straight crap. George is almost bald. He tries everything from prayer to poultices to keep it, but nothing works."

I meet her as she crosses the room and give her a big hug. "Hello Charlene. How have you been? How's the family these days?"

"Well nobody's crazy enough for the loony bin yet. But it's just a matter of time of course. You know few families in the South send their crazy folks away; they keep them at home so they can trot them out on Sundays and put them on the front porch for everybody to see. It's sort of a badge of honor. We don't have our nutcase yet, but we're still working hard at it. As you know, momma is always doing her best to drive at least one of us over the edge."

Charlene takes off her sunglasses and sits down at the kitchen table. Most everyone gravitates to the kitchen table, especially family visitors. She looks around for the coffee pot, gets up, pours a mug from the omnipresent coffee maker and returns to her chair.

"Honey, you know in the South, the next best thing to a crazy in the family is an alcoholic. We're doubly blessed because we're real close to having two of them. Bubba Jerry and his namby-pamby wife Susanne still drink all the time."

"I thought they were getting better when I left." I said.

"Oh honey, they've been on and off the wagon so many times in the last five years you'd have to have a calculator to keep up."

"I'm sorry to hear that, but I'm not at all surprised."

She takes a sip of coffee and continues. "I can't say that I blame them though. They've had so much trouble with that floozy daughter of theirs, Pauline. She and the 'high-yeller' baby she had two years ago have almost driven them out of their minds. You know she's had three bastard children over the years."

I can't help registering my astonishment. "Oh my god, not another one?"

"I thought you knew. Of course, she gave the first two up for adoption. When she got pregnant with the last one, she was hell-bent on keeping it. So when it came out like the 'Tar Baby', Bubba and Suzanne couldn't talk her into getting rid of it."

Charlene pauses to take a breath and another sip from the mug. "Momma, of course was fit to be tied. She couldn't understand why, she didn't at least kept one of the *white* ones. She will not acknowledge the baby's existence. The day after it was born, she went to the lawyer's office and wrote her out of the family."

"That sounds just like something I would expect from Clairisse." I added while Charlene was snatching another sip of coffee.

"At first, Bubba and Suzanne refused to have anything to do with her in an effort to force her to give it up for adoption. They tell everybody his daddy is an Indian, you know, one of those curry people, not the teepee kind. But it doesn't make any difference what they call him. When they all come back to Kellersville to visit, they make her husband or *whatever* he is come in the back door so the neighbors will think he's the yard man."

She pauses just long enough to take another swallow from the mug in her left hand and continues her monologue while making a gesture of resignation with the right palm turned up and a shrug of the shoulder. "George and I don't know exactly what to say or do. You know *we* are not prejudiced. *However* they want to live their lives is not for us to judge. We just hate how it affects Momma. Of course when she finds out they're coming to town she starts to have the vapors. She takes serious sick and family suppers are definitely cancelled until after they've gone. Thank the Lord they don't come much."

I had forgotten the price paid for open-ended, general questions to Charlene. Even those seemingly simple inquiries requesting just a "yes/no" response were dangerous if one lost control of the conversation. Charlene tells all. Most frequently more than anyone wants to know or wants anyone else to know for that matter.

"And speaking of family dinners, Momma says to remind you that everyone comes at five thirty just like always. She is expecting you and PK for supper tomorrow evening."

"Charlene, this is very short notice. I've already made plans to be here tomorrow night."

Slapping her forehead with her palm and popping her neck backwards with her eyes rolling to the ceiling, Charlene moans, "Oh sweet Jesus! Momma's got her head set on it and you know what *that* means. You'll have to call her and tell her yourself. I'll be damned if I going to piss her off again this morning. My day has already started off bad enough without having to tell her you're turning down Sunday dinner. You know Momma doesn't take no for an answer without a struggle. She'll take it out on us and make our lives miserable all evening. Are you sure you won't change your mind? Just come on and get it over with."

All the years of dealing with Clairisse flash through my mind. Even though I feel compassion for Charlene who will have to relay the message, I find the courage to reply, "Charlene, she sent her invitation (I wanted to say command) by messenger and my reply will be returned in the same manner. I don't know why she is so eager to summon me now. When I lived here I was not usually invited, even through the back door. I'm sure she'll lose interest and forget it once I've been here a few days. She'll ask enough times to be polite and avoid the certain criticism from Belle's beauties."

"I don't know Harper. I'm not sure what it is, but she's got something up her sleeve. You remember how she gets when she sets her mind. Nothing and nobody rests until . . . well, you know what I mean. It's just not natural the way she dogs a thing or a body to death until she gets her way. Sometimes it's just easier to just give up at the beginning and save a lot of grief."

"Yes, I remember only too well. What is it now?" I asked. "What could possibly be so important to summon me after not having heard a single word from her in five years, not that we had much contact before I left town. I always thought Clairisse suspected my secret and because of her Christian upbringing couldn't deal with having a queer in such a fine, old, respectable family. At least the black man is allowed in the house even if it was through the servant's entrance."

"Harper, you're not being fair. You know how hard it is for Momma to deal with people who are—well—you know—different! We just have to accept her for herself. After all, she's getting old."

"That's a bunch of crap Charlene. She's always been that way and you know it. I don't want to get into all this right now. I have more serious and important things on my plate. Just thank her for the invitation and let it go at that. And speaking of going, I have a lot of errands to run and I need to go. Say hello to your family."

Seven

Curiosity Killed the Cat—
Satisfaction Brought It Back to Life

The night has been sleepless for everyone. I toss and turn trying to weigh all the options. In addition, I can't sleep because I hear PK crying until late. Hank has paced several hours on the porch. Only Nan sleeps soundly thanks to the medication.

Sunday mornings in a sleepy Southern town offer only two options, coffee with the Sunday paper and a leisurely breakfast or church. The latter can turn out to be an all-day affair especially when there's dinner on the ground to celebrate such special occasions as "homecoming," the annual reunion when people who have moved, return for preaching and to catch up with the latest gossip or family news.

My serenity is broken by the telephone. "Dad, it's for you. I think it might be Aunt Clairisse." PK whispers as he places his hand over the receiver. "Wonder what she wants?"

I sense my eyes are rolling like an out-of-control merry-go-round as I take the phone from PK. "Hello." PK's identification is correct.

"Harper, honey, welcome home."

Calmly I respond, "Well Clairisse, what a surprise to hear your voice after all this time. It's been so long, I barely recognized you." I fight my urge to hang up the receiver and run for cover from the anticipated lightening strike to punish my audacious lie. I would never fail to identify her rasp. Once you've heard the voice of Satan, it's burned in your memory for eternity.

"Sweetheart, I heard you were in town and just couldn't wait to see you. I sent Charlene over to ask you and PK to our family supper tonight. I was just devastated to hear y'all already had other plans. We're just dying to get you two around our family table again. Are you sure y'all can't make it?"

"Actually Clairisse, we are planning dinner here. I just got here and Hank has so little free time during the football season. Sundays are just about the only time he has for a family dinner. Maybe some other time. I'll be here for awhile."

"Oh?" she drawls out and waits for an explanation. When none is forthcoming, she continues, "This must be a special occasion. You haven't spent any time here in five years." Again she pauses to give me an opportunity to offer information.

In a diabolical fashion, I actually enjoy the cat 'n mouse game. It gives me a feeling of power, especially since I know how much it must have galled her to call and pick for information. I really want to drag it out and make her fish for the details or better still, tell someone at Belle's and let Clairisse suffer the humiliation of finding out second hand from a non-family member. But in the short time I create by stalling, I decide not to use Nan's illness as a means of retaliation against Clairisse, no matter how tempting it might be.

After enough time elapses to continue the suspense of whether or not I am going to relent and offer any information, I continued. "Nan went to Birmingham to the Medical Center last week. They diagnosed her with pancreatic cancer. She has only a very short time. Hank and PK need help during this time and I came to do what I can."

"Oh hon-ney, I'm so sor-ry. I knew she wasn't doing well. Of course, you couldn't miss that she was sick. Bless her heart, her color and all just gave it away. I saw her at the drug store the other day and I told Suzanne and Charlene it was more than diabetes. How are Hank and PK holding up?"

I can tell by the tone of her voice she already knows all the details and that I have been suffering under a stupid delusion thinking I am in control of the conversation. She has been manipulating me all along. Knowing the grapevine in Kellersville, the test results probably got back to Belle's before Hank and Nan returned from Birmingham.

"They're doing fine considering. Of course they are very shocked that the time is so short," I pitched in. Clairisse's failure to ask how much time was evidence enough that she most likely knew before I did.

This stirs my curiosity. I want to know more because I am convinced she has something working in her devious little mind. It'll be hard waiting for her to reveal her intentions. However, it is critical I not ask any leading questions given that Clairisse is known to lie rather than expose her plan before her chosen moment.

In order to get as close to the real truth as possible, details will have to be sifted and analyzed. I certainly don't want to cloud the situation with preempted details designed to hide the real issue. This lesson, learned through many years of experience, is still etched in my memory. The best course of action is to wait.

Again, I have to admit I have been outmaneuvered and my moment in the driver's seat has been like a teenager sitting in an expensive sports car on the showroom floor, only a daydream. Nothing has changed. As usual, Clairisse is in control.

I know PK and I will eventually have to show up at the family repast so I decide on preemptive action and ask for a rain check. "What about next Sunday"?

"That will be wonderful. We're so anxious to see you. Everybody'll be so disappointed y'all aren't coming tonight."

"I'll try to drop by for a quick hello this week."

"Please do. I'll be real glad to see you."

Why is she so intent to contact me so soon? After all, neither of us has made the slightest attempt at communication during my five-year absence. The simple fact is, both of us will have to wait until next Sunday.

Eight

After I'm Gone

"What a gorgeous day for this time of the year." Nan sits down in the porch swing next to me. On the screened porches of small Southern towns, there is always a metal glider or a white wood-slat swing suspended from the ceiling by two lengths of chain. The effect of sitting in the swing is a sure-fire guarantee to loosen the tongue of even the most inhibited. I can't remember how many hours Nan and I have spent in this very spot. Here in the quietness of our refuge from what we once called the hurly burly of our lives, we have cussed and discussed many problems; none, however, with so dire consequences as the monster that now faces our family.

She begins to speak in a low voice to avoid being overheard by PK or Hank. "Harper, I need to talk to you about the future—not mine of course, we know what that is."

"Nan, I don't know if I can do this now."

"If not now, when?"

I lowered my head. "You know I love you so much. All our lives, you've watched out for me and protected me during the hardest of times. Five years ago, you selflessly gave me a new life. Now, I want to do the same for you and I am powerless."

"You can give me the peace of mind to die knowing that you are here to support and guide PK and Hank through these last months. You *can* do this and I know you will be stronger than you think when the situations arise."

"I just hate for PK to have to deal with this. It is going to put a big burden on his emotions and I hope he can survive with as few scars as possible."

"I'm sure you and PK will make a good team. He's young and is stronger than you give him credit for. I'm not as concerned about him as I am about Hank."

"Why are you worried about Hank?"

"I just hope Hank can get out of this town. He and I were making plans to look for other jobs for next year. We feel so culturally stifled and imprisoned here."

"I certainly understand that feeling, especially after having lived the last five years away from Kellersville. It's like getting out of an emotional prison to live in an accepting environment where you are not judged by the ideological standards of bigots and bubbas."

"Yes, we are both aware there is an outside world. Since I'll never escape, I will die easier if I know PK and Hank are going to have a chance to break out. Hank is a great math teacher and he can easily get a job almost anywhere. I don't want PK to grow up in this environment. He never seems to entirely fit in, even with his best friends."

"I don't know what I can do. Hank's a grown man. He'll make his own decisions. I'm sure he'll find the best place for himself. I certainly feel the same way about Kellersville. I'm so glad I got out." I instantly realize the implications of my remark. "I didn't mean away from you and PK."

"I know that, sweetie." Nan hastens to reassure me. "I also know Hank doesn't have the strength to make that type of decision. With my death and PK leaving, he will opt for the easiest answer. He'll just stay here and be miserable until retirement. All I want you to do is support him and give him a big push on the road out of town. He's always liked you and since you have been here, he's begun to depend on your strength, just like PK and I have done for ever."

"I'll do the best I can."

"That's all I ask."

Nine

When You're Hot, You're Hot!

In my opinion, a PTA meeting was, is and always will be a rash on a teacher's butt. Parental involvement in the educational process is the life blood of student success. These punch-'n-cookies gatherings after a long day of teaching, however, are another story. They are little more than social get-togethers and are rarely as effective as organized small-group meetings with a definite purpose and result in mind.

Nan, however, is of the opposite opinion. She is an ardent participant and never misses. Tonight's meeting, however, is going to be the first time she has failed to show up as either a teacher or parent. She starts moaning early in the morning about having to forego the assembly and especially the face-to-face conferences with PK's teachers.

Finally after several hours of her not-so-subtle hints such as leaving the PTA calendar on the kitchen table with today's date circled in red and in the circle the word CAKE printed with stars, she ventures a casual comment.

"This is the second Tuesday of the month." She doesn't even raise her eyes from the magazine she is thumbing through.

"Oh?" I respond dreading to hear her next comment which I know with certainty will follow. In the last five years, I have easily gotten accustomed to the absence of this drudgery and certainly don't have the slightest desire to pick up where I so joyfully left off.

"The PTA meeting is tonight."

"Is that so?"

"You can't have forgotten how important it is to keep in touch with what's going on at school."

"I haven't forgotten what a pain-in-the-ass they are and I certainly don't miss them."

She pretends to ignore my comments. "I was thinking it would be a wonderful opportunity for you to rekindle your collegial ties with everybody at school. I'm sure they are all anxious to see you."

"First of all, you *know* how much I *hate* these things. As for keeping a finger on current happenings, this is Kellersville; nobody has to go to a PTA meeting to find out what's going on."

"But we need to be involved with PK's classes.

Finally, I relent and agree to go to the meeting. "I want you to realize this is the *ultimate* in sacrifices. Do I have to take a cake or cookies?"

"It's already in a cake box on the counter next to the refrigerator."

"You were so sure of your persuasive powers. What if I had refused?"

"I had a back-up plan."

"And that was…?"

"I'll just save it until next time."

When I walk in the front door of the school, my mind begins a frantic and erratic instant replay of past events of both my years as a student and tenure as a teacher. Looking around, I briefly imagine I'm sixteen again. I glance to my left and feel goose bumps when I can see all the way into the principal's office through the school secretary's door which, open as always on such occasions, reproduces mental images of the greater part of my entire life. I fight the urge to turn and run; it's too much too quickly. I'm still having trouble adjusting to Nan's impending death and returning to a part of life I long considered past is unnerving to say the least. Thankfully, I don't make the mistake of thinking there is any reasonable recourse at this juncture. I'll have to swallow the bitter pill and do the best I can.

"Why, Harper Wolfe. What a pleasant surprise!" Walking directly toward me is Peter Aslov, the chemistry teacher to many generations of Kellersville's finest. When I hear the familiar accent, I jog my memory to remember exactly where he is from. It is generally thought he migrated from an iron-curtain country to escape the communist regime. In any event, he's an institution at Kellersville High School and a welcome sight in this environment which is starting to engulf me. Mr. Aslov— I could never bring myself to call him Peter even after several years as a colleague— had been one of my favorites as both teacher and lunch companion in the faculty lounge.

"Mr. Aslov. Thank God for a friendly face!" I extend my hand, but Mr. Aslov embraces me in a hug that both surprises and pleases one of his biggest fans.

"How's Nan?"

"About the same, thank you."

"Mrs. A (In forty-six years of marriage, he had never called Salina by her given name; just Mrs. A) was over last week and said you were coming. She said Nan was glad to have you home for awhile, even though, you know..."

I quickly, if not smoothly, changed the subject. "Nan saved me some of the matzo ball soup. It was delicious as usual. Salina's matzo balls can't be beat."

"This is my last year. I've decided it's time for me to become inert."

"I don't believe it. I can't imagine Kellersville High without you. Is your health alright?" I immediately feel a flush on my cheeks from the embarrassment by my presumptuous familiarity with someone I still can't address by his given name. "Do you have any plans? What will you do?"

"Whatever. And yes, my health is still great. I just want to stop while I can possibly enjoy some leisure time."

At that moment, the bell announces the activities are about to start in the auditorium.

"They're off and running! You know how much I hate these meetings. I can't wait until I don't have to attend another one! You asked me what I'm going to do. Well I damn sure know what I'm *not* going to do. But for now, let's go kiddo!"

The general meeting of the Kellersville PTA will be forever the same; more boring than watching owl shit dry! The twenty-minute ordeal always ends with the instructions for parents to follow their child's individual schedule and visit each class in turn.

I automatically go through PK's class routine with as much interest and as many smiles as I can muster; I dread the fifth period; the class that will put me face to face with Nan's replacement. I have not heard anything about her. In fact, until the program started, it had not even occurred to me the situation would arise.

Ina Collier was a native of Illinois. Chicago born and raised, she attended Northwestern where she majored in History and finished her MS with a specialty in American History. She had married during graduate school to a friend of many years. Although the friendship had weathered the storms of many years, the marriage didn't fare as well; he was a sexual butterfly, a fact she suspected throughout the years, but discarded in the hopes of making the marriage work. Finally after she became aware of several of his side interests, she decided to call a halt. She dropped the final papers filing for a divorce and application for the job in Kellersville in the mailbox at the same time. It was time for her to start a new life in a new and different place.

As I enter Nan's old classroom, I have to grab the door jamb for support; my weak knees and dizziness cause me to immediately turn to escape. Too late! From the outside of my body, I hear a pleasant, but high-pitched Yankee twang coming from behind me.

"Hello! If you're looking for American History, this is the right place."

I turn and face a well-groomed slim woman with graying-blonde hair; at least she is letting the colors blend naturally. There is a minimum of makeup and her outfit is tailored and professional. I can tell immediately she's comfortable in the classroom and the parent-teacher conference environment. She extends her hand in a gentle welcoming motion.

"Well, I guess this is the place." I say and pray she didn't notice the cliché. I hope I've managed to camouflage my flush of embarrassment at having seemed to be lost or worse, being caught in the act of flight. "I'm PK's dad."

"Somehow, I would have managed to figure that out even if I hadn't recognized your picture from the dust jackets of your books. I know most of my students' fathers. Besides, you were fingered when you came in the auditorium. Have you so quickly forgotten the features of living in a small town?"

"I'm remembering minute by minute."

"I'm Ina Collier, Nan's substitute."

I'm instantly impressed by her sensitivity at avoiding the use of the word "replacement," and have the feeling it would be easy to sit and chat. But since there are other parents in the room and the plan for the night's events doesn't include individual conferences, there is no opportunity to linger. At the end of the designated ten-minute period, I offer the habitual parent comment, "I'm very pleased to meet you. Please contact us if there is anything we need to know regarding PK's studies."

Ten

"Study" Clubs

The PTA meeting is over by eight-fifteen. As I return home and enter Nan's room, I hear her saying, "Yes Mrs. Dobbins. We'll be here tomorrow afternoon and I'm sure Harper will be delighted to see you." She turns to me and, with the slight toss of her head, which I recall as a sign of resignation, relays the message. "That was Mrs. Charles Dobbins."

"*The* Mrs. Dobbins of, My-husband-the banker fame?"

"The one and only, in the flesh, and these days lots of it. She wants to drop by and visit for a few minutes." Nodding her head, Nan continues, "I have a strong hunch she is going to invite you to be the guest speaker at her study club this month. She is moving quickly so you won't get another invitation before she can claim an exclusive."

"Oh my God! I had forgotten about the old-lady 'sororities.' Surely they're not still doing *those* gossip sessions."

"Every third Thursday night of the month, without fail," Nan confirmed with a roll of the eyes.

"There is nothing I'd rather do than tell that old biddy to shove it. However, I really do this all the time on book tours and I suppose I should do it here as well – just one of the responsibilities of all us literary whores."

The next afternoon at precisely two o'clock, I make my way through the living room to the front door as soon as I hear the sound of a car in the drive. A slag driveway is almost as good as an early warning radar system or a barking dog.

The "study clubs," as they are called in an attempt to give some credibility to small-town hen sessions, have been fixtures in Kellersville since before my time. In the forties after the war, there was a rash of Kellersville men returning with brides from strange places. Some of them were not only from outside the South, but from other countries, the ultimate disgrace. The reactions from the home-town folk were pure disbelief that anyone of these native sons of Kellersville would look beyond their childhood neighbors for friends, not to speak of life partners. These new arrivals and an inborn distrust of all outsiders, prompted protective walls of social rejection.

Harry Singleton had returned with a lovely British girl who is still regarded as a foreigner. She did, however, enjoy a higher social acceptability than Mildred Atkins, the Yankee implant from Ohio. Les Dames, Mrs. Dobbins' study club, was the snootiest and most exclusive of the gaggle. Their charter was written to exclude anyone not fortunate enough to be born and raised in the bosom of culture.

There are twelve members; one for each month's meeting. Guests are allowed but only if on a list approved in advance by the associates. There is a prescribed format for the meetings and although the designated literary work frequently takes a back seat to the current item of social minutia, each member is expected to read the month's selection and be ready to discuss it in depth.

"Mrs. Dobbins, you've not changed a bit." Of course I was lying through my teeth, an art every Southerner learns before the end of kindergarten. She had, just as Nan had described, gone up at least three dress sizes. "Do come on in. Would you like some tea?" Southern custom dictates that refreshments are always offered but rarely accepted until at least the second or third mention. It was considered ill mannered to avail oneself of any liquid exchange, in or out, until seated at least ten minutes.

"No thank you darling. It's so nice to see you again Harper. You're just as good looking and charming as ever. Life seems to be agreeing with you. Where is it you are living now? I read on the dust jacket of your last book you were in California, Palm Springs, I believe. I'll just pop in on Nan for a few moments before we have our little chat."

I hear the screen door opening and see Hank coming in the kitchen. I meet him with a warning whisper. "It's the Dobbins woman."

"What the hell does she want? I've never seen her on this side of town. It must be something important."

"Me!" I grinned.

"I can't say that I blame her. You look especially dashing in that sweater. Where did you get it?" queried Hank with a knowing smile.

"From your closet— I needed something to keep off the chill. Nan said you wouldn't mind. It's a little loose in the arms and shoulders though. I guess I'll have to work out a little extra if I want to continue borrowing your clothes." I give Hank a little tap on the arm.

Without hesitation Hank jabs back. "No use trying to borrow my jeans; they'd be loose in the …" When Hank realizes what he has just said, he begins to blush from the tips of his toes to the Bama cap on his head.

The embarrassment of the moment is mercifully broken by Nan's voice calling. "Bring Mrs. Dobbins a cup of tea and come on in the bedroom. The water is still hot on the stove."

Turning toward the stove, I see that Hank has slipped out of the room. After preparing a tray with three cups, sugar cubes, milk and some Walker's shortbread cookies, I take a deep breath and go to hear what has brought the dowager of Les Dames to visit the other side of town.

"Harper, we are so thrilled you've finally come back to Kellersville. Of course [glancing at Nan], we're just devastated at the circumstances. Anyway, we can't pass up the opportunity to ask our own best-selling author to allow Les Dames to host him at our meeting next Thursday night. Even before you arrived, we had put *Death Comes To Call* on this month's reading list. We never dreamed we'd ever have this occasion presented at the very time we were reading the actual novel. It's just so exciting! May we put your name in the paper as our guest?"

Repressing the urge to cause a bigger ripple than a turd in punchbowl, I accept. "Mrs. Dobbins, it will be a distinct pleasure."

"Oh Harper, I am ecstatic. I just can't wait to tell the committee. I'll send you a note with the details. Lovely, lovely—just lovely!" She rises to leave without acknowledging the cup of tea on the table next to her chair. Neither of us dares to mention the refreshments for fear she will sit back down. An untouched cup of cold tea is not a problem. An extension of her stay is!

I try to hide the haste with which I usher the grand dame out the door. As I walk into the den where Hank relaxes in his recliner, I think of the aging actress' famous words upon being released from a two-month cure, "I'm glad that shit's over. Somebody get me a drink."

Eleven

The Prodigal Son

I am relieved when the appointed Thursday night finally arrives. I am usually never nervous over these appearances, but tonight's book signing is different. I'm the home-town boy returning. Twelve of the snootiest and pickiest of Kellersville self-proclaimed upper crust would be there waiting for a brilliant presentation. Generally, I'm not at all impressed by these social wannabes, but, in this situation, I have to admit their approval and admiration are important to me. It's like a child who can finally show off in front of all the grown ups.

As Hank enters the kitchen, I look up from the notes I have been jotting on the five-by-eight note cards I always use on these occasions. Although there is a standard format I use, I always try to include something peculiar to the current situation and group I'm addressing. When I first sat down to prepare, I thought this would be difficult since I haven't had any personal contact with these women in years. But once I start, the memories begin to roll in and out of my mind so fast they're overlapping. The truth is, I'm having a hard time editing my thoughts. I don't want to leave anyone out of my walk down the avenue of fond recollections. Of course there are those memories I will push back into the drawer of my long-term remembrances, much to the relief of all involved.

I decide to catch him before I miss the opportunity. "Hi! How's your day been?

"Not bad. Yours?"

"Hank, I need a favor from you. Tonight's the presentation at Les Dames. Since I turned in the rental car, I'll need you to take me and pick me up. If you want to stay for my performance, I'm sure they will be happy to have so young and good-looking a stud to adorn the stage."

Hank smiles at being referred to as a stud, especially by another male. "No thank you! You can borrow the truck. I won't need it tonight."

"I can't drive a stick. I never learned. Besides, with you there, it will be easier to bring it to a close. I don't want to stay any longer than I have to."

"I'll teach you."

"You'll take me!" When I realize just how bossy that had sounded, I begin to rouge up like a country-club president's wife who farts as she stands to read the menu for the annual Ladies Auxiliary luncheon. The entire exchange resembles far too much a little family spat. I steal a furtive glance at Hank who obviously has not perceived it in that manner and has taken it in stride.

"Okay, I'll take you, but I won't stay. I'll go have a beer and come back to pick you up at eight."

"Whatever you say. You can bring me a beer when you pick me up. I'll need something to relax afterwards."

Later, when Hank comes downstairs, he looks especially spiffy. It is obvious he has changed and fixed up for something. He usually doesn't go to this trouble for the Hog's Trough. Maybe he's meeting friends. It surely isn't a girl friend, not that any of the honky-tonk types at the local watering hole would pass up the chance to jump in the sack with him. The fact is, Hank isn't the unfaithful type.

Neither of us speaks until we reach the bank. Although the hostess role shifts from month to month, they always use the board room at the bank for their meetings.

As I open the car door to get out, Hank says, "I changed my mind. I might as well see what you're all about." I feel my head swelling and as we walk up to the front entrance, I suck in my gut and put on my best grin. I want my personality and achievement to shine especially brightly tonight.

Sarah Cawthon Threadgood, affectionately known as Miss Sally, is the hostess for this month's meeting. She has dutifully positioned herself at the door to officially welcome all members and guests.

"Har-wa-pur, I'm just so thrilled to see you again looking so good just like you've not even aged these past …*gasp*… years like the rest of us. [Her style of speaking in run-on sentences causes considerable apprehension to one who is hearing her for the first time. She breaks only to draw an almost hysterical breath which sounds like the payment cylinder being sucked through one of those old-fashion vacuum systems in the department stores of the Forties and Fifties. The randomness of the inhalations causes difficulty in understanding her until one gets used to it.] We just can't tell you how honored we are to …*gasp*… have you here to address our little study club. Of course, we just adore all …*gasp*… your books. Whenever a new one comes out, we just scurry on down to Peterson's …*gasp*… Drug Store and order fourteen, one for each of us and the school and public library." …*gasp*

"My agent and I really appreciate that Miss Sally. PK's going to college soon and every little bit helps."

"He's such a sweet boy. How's he dealing with Nan's illness?"

"He's doing real well with it considering he's only a teenager."

"That's good. And Hank, I'm delighted to see the football coach here to soak up some …*gasp*… culture from our artist in residence. We're so proud of him you know (nodding in my direction). We all feel just like he's …*gasp*… our son. I especially sense a close bond with him since I was his …*gasp*… sophomore English teacher and the first to realize his vast potential as a…*gasp*…writer. And, of course, I was hoping he would come back to Kellersville to take my place when I got…*gasp*… old and was ready to be put out in the retirement pasture, but, alas, 'Old Man Warren' gave out before I did. At least I got …*gasp*…to work with him for two years. What a pleasure to be able to see such a great liter… *gasp*…ary mind at work, although I'm sure none of the students ever really appreciated what…*gasp*… they had. I remember when Bill Warren first started teaching. He depended on…*gasp*… me to tell him which end of the book to start with. Poor thing, he never really seemed to get himself organized."

I laughed so heartily to myself I almost let my amusement slip out in a loud guffaw. It was generally assumed that Mr. Warren had been *born* old. I really don't know anyone who remembers him otherwise. It's well-known that Mr. Warren and Miss Sally dated for several years at the beginning of his tenure at Kellersville High School. In fact, everyone assumed they would eventually make it official. Although no one was ever sure what happened to their relationship, the not-so-low-key feud caused by the schism became the feed of the gossip geese for many years to come. In fact, many students played the warring ex-lovers against each other in order to gain some academic advantage or special favor.

"Please come in. I'd say I'd introduce you, but there's …*gasp*… nobody here you don't already know. We decided to be selfish and keep you all …*gasp*… to ourselves so there are no guests here tonight, except for Hank and you…*gasp*… certainly know him. Madame …*gasp*… Chairlady, it is with great pleasure that I present to you our honoree for the evenin', Mister …*gasp*… Har-wa-pur **Lee**-raw-ree Wolfe." …*gasp*

Hearing the standard Southern pronunciation of Leroy, the middle name I inherited from my grandfather, always has and I guess always will send chills down my spine like hearing fingernails scraping on a chalky blackboard. I hate the sound of it so much I have threatened for years to have it legally changed to Lee, the abbreviated form Nan and I gave PK as a tribute to the Johnson clan, mother's paternal family. I make a mental note to do just that while I'm here in Alabama.

Mrs. Dobbins approaches with her hand extended in a palm-down position as if she is expecting me to kiss it in the gallant style of the Old South. I'm convinced many citizens of Kellersville have done a lot of kissing in the past. I'm equally sure, however, that her hand was not involved.

"Mr. Wolfe, welcome to our study club. We've been eagerly anticipating this evening and are elated you are finally here."

As she turns toward the other members to begin the formal introduction of the evening's program, Hank puts his hand to his mouth and mutters under his breath "I haven't seen so much shit since the *honey wagon* from the renovation construction site at the Civic Center turned over in the ditch last August. Needless to say, the summer heat and humidity made it a memorable occasion for us all."

"Ladies, let's all take our places. Mr. Warner, we weren't expecting you this evening so we don't have you a seat reserved in the front. I hope you won't be offended by sitting in that chair in the rear. [Hank smiles and gladly moves toward the back row.] The meeting of the *Les Dames* study club will come to order. Will the Secretary please read the minutes of the last meeting?"

As they continue with the plastic formalities, I take this final opportunity to glance around the room to review the remaining top ten of Kellersville society. At first I'm surprised Clairisse isn't among the membership. Then I remember she was born in Dawson's Ditch, only eight miles from Kellersville, but it might as well have been eight hundred—she was *not* a Kellersville native.

How could I have forgotten that famous incident ten years ago? It was definitely the talk of the jaw-bones for almost a month. After years of being ignored by the *crème de la* crème, Clairisse took every opportunity to oppose the snooty members—especially the grand dame. Once, as the owner of *Polly's Pansy* Patch, Kellersville's solitary flower shop which Clairisse had purchased after her husband's death to lock in the funeral business in that region of the county, Clairisse had Mr. Dobbins' birthday arrangement to his wife, Gladys, changed to a funeral spray with "For Your Special Day" glittered on the purple ribbon. The following day, the recipient sent a note: "Hopefully I can return the sentiment before the arrangement gives out. As always, Gladys."

My attention springs back to the dais when I hear my name announced. I stand and make my way to the front of the room accompanied by a muted but enthusiastic ovation; twenty-four gloved hands don't make much sound.

"Good evening ladies. First I would like to thank Mrs. Dobbins, your president, for inviting me this evening. It is a real honor to be here. And to our hostess, Mrs. Threadgood, you certainly seem to have outdone yourselves with the flowers and the food. As I came in, I noticed that beautiful display of goodies and can't wait to sample a few of them.

When I was thinking about what to say tonight, I asked myself 'What will I say'? Then quickly, the answer came to me. This is my home. You are my people and I am your product. Each of you has contributed to my life." I continue moving around the room and relating a short personal anecdote about each lady. When I finish my speech about writing my first novel *Dying to be Different*, I look into the audience and announce, "Ladies if there are any questions, I will be proud to answer them to the best of my ability. But I warn you, if any of your queries regards the apple pie that went missing from Mrs. Rutherford's sideboard in late summer before my ninth grade year, I don't remember a thing."

The entire group howls. Mrs. Rutherford stands part way in her seat and says, "I suspected you were the guilty party when your mother came over the next day to borrow some baking soda to ease your bellyache. I never said a word about it. I assumed you had paid for your crime." She giggles as she sits back down.

Helen Barnes raises her gloved hand. Famous for over accessorizing, many say she has to wear it all because she doesn't own a jewelry box. So when her hand shoots upward, there is a clanging noise from all the bracelets collecting toward her elbow. The accompanying titters from around the room go seemingly unnoticed by Helen who is now on the edge of her chair ready to ask the first question.

"Miss Helen, what's on your mind this evening?"

"I was just wondering who the models for your characters were? Some of us feel like we deserve a little of the royalties."

I can hardly suppress. "Which character did you identify with Miss Helen? I certainly hope it wasn't the corpse!" The room breaks up.

Miss Laura Belle Miller, the oldest of the group, chirrups in "That's my role, Helen. I've been rehearsing that part for years now. You'll have to wait your turn."

The giggles add a pleasant informality.

"Actually, a writer always creates his characters from all the people he knows. But it's rarely only one particular person. Besides, Miss Helen, you're too pretty and sweet. None of my characters would want to do away with you."

"Harper, you always were able to charm the snakes right out of the depths of hell. You haven't changed a bit!"

As the customary signal that the program is over, Mrs. Dobbins rises. She cocks her head to the right and extends both hands toward me in a palm-down gesture. As she approaches, she lightly clasps her hands together in semi-prayerful position and as she opens them she clutches them to her chest. "My dear Harper, you have far surpassed our expectations for the evening. May we offer you some light refreshment?"

My first thought is to look for the scotch bottle—foolish boy! Almost immediately I notice Miss Helen maneuvering her walker in a bee line toward the food table. My gaze follows her to her destination which I can't help but notice contains only a meager offering of sandwiches, cookies, cheese dip and crackers—it's almost as if no one expects the food to be touched. As I continue to stare as unobtrusively as possible, a most curious spectacle played out in front of my eyes. She positions her walker next to the table, sits on the little platform, spreads a napkin on her lap and proceeds to dine. She uses one cracker for three scoops in the onion dip. While sticking her fingers into the dish to retrieve a piece of the second cracker which breaks as she drags it through the dish, a glob falls on the table. She scoops it up with her finger and licks it clean—well almost. Since the charms of her granny bracelet have caught more of the dip than the cracker, she raises her wrist and swabs her tongue over the baubles failing to notice her elbow plowing into the dish in the process.

When I look around, I see everyone in the entire room, including Hank, is apparently paying absolutely no attention to the scene which has reduced my appetite to a minus ten on the hunger scale. Am I the only one witnessing this etiquette nightmare? Even the table attendant seems to be totally unaware of the sloppiness being displayed by one of Kellersville's elite. Surely Emily Post is taking a spin, wherever she has ended up.

I continue to be transfixed by this spectacle like a drooling hound dog waiting for his master to offer him the platter of gnawed rib bones at the end of the picnic table. Miss Helen reaches for a chicken salad sandwich. She takes two, discards the top slices of the neatly crust-trimmed triangles and puts them together to make a fatter nibble. She carefully puts the two discarded triangles together to form a meatless shell and replaces them on the table making it appear she has taken only one.

After five or six minutes of stuffing herself, she daintily wipes her lips, stands and begins pushing her rolling walker to join a group of women in the corner. As soon as her back is turned, the table is cleared of food and a new selection of food is arranged on a pristine and starched tablecloth. Even the centerpiece is replaced. Almost immediately, others approach the refreshments and start to partake. Suddenly, It comes to me that I am the only one in the room who is ignorant of the routine. Even Hank has waited for Miss Helen to finish. Being away from Kellersville for so long has left me totally unaware of the latest local eccentricities. It is a very strange sensation to be an outsider in my own hometown.

The meeting was a complete success. I felt at the same time brilliantly literary and personally reminiscent. The "dames" were sufficiently captivated, but I could have cared less. It was Hank I wanted to impress.

When we got into the truck, Hank reached over and grabbed my shoulder. "I think you deserve a beer."

I melt inside with both euphoria and guilt. After all, this is Nan's husband.

Twelve

An Old Friend Comes to the Rescue

During these past two weeks, I come to realize that caring for Nan, PK and the house is going to demand all my strength and courage. PK hasn't been able to talk about his fears and has walked around in a funk. At the outset, he was understandably moody and wanted to stay home from school. We decided to allow it, but began to insist he go back after a few days. Even though he is getting better at controlling his emotions during the waking hours when activities and friends occupy his mind, he frequently cries himself to sleep only to wake and repeat the cycle several times a night. The first time I heard him, I started into his room to console him.

"Harper," Nan speaks to me through her open bedroom door, "will you come in for just a second?"

I notice Hank grading papers in the overstuffed chair next to the window. My thoughts rage through time to the nights I spent in that very chair reading essays and complaining about the irreverence students demonstrated for punctuation and grammar. I feel a sagging sensation in my stomach; I can't decide if it is melancholy or jealousy at seeing Hank in what had been my sacred corner for so many years.

"I might have known you two would still be up."

Hank looks up from the pile of papers in his lap. "This is the only time I have to get them corrected. They won't go away by themselves."

Nan laughs. "I could never seem to lose them no matter how hard I tried. I'm sure they'll send me a set to mark on the way to the crematorium."

"I certainly don't miss that chore," I said.

"Were you going in to console PK?"

"Yes. I was very concerned."

"He's got to deal with this in his own time and own way. It's taking all I can do to stay in here. Besides, I think he would be a little embarrassed if he knew we could hear him."

"Whatever you think. I just wanted to help."

"I think it's best this way."

I am beginning to sense frustration in not being able to console PK. In addition, I'm bending under the pressure from my feeling of inadequacy to handle Nan's day-to-day medical needs. The possibility of making an error that would cost precious time in the struggle to maintain a quality of life for Nan during the final weeks is terrifying. I know there will come a time when she will have to be hospitalized, but I want to prolong the inevitable for all concerned.

Hiring some competent help seems the only plausible answer. The question, however, is where to look in this small country town. Normally one goes to family for suggestions. The price of Clairisse's involvement is too high to pay. Hiring someone suggested by Clairisse would not only give her a mole in the house and a direct pipeline to their most intimate moments, but also a sense of control that must be avoided at all costs. Keeping her from finding out about my employing someone will be impossible. The only hope is to do it before it becomes cut 'n curl fodder at the local beauty on a budget.

I take Nan's advice and go to my room and try to sleep. It's easier now that I have finally made the decision to get some help.

The next morning, I decide to contact the hospital for possible leads to hire a practical nurse or sitter. As I set out for the short walk to pick up Nan's medicine at Petersen's, I determine to stop over at the local hospital on the way back from the pharmacy, which is in the same block.

The air is crisp and bright. A slight breeze passes gently through the branches of the old oaks lining the street. Sidewalks were never considered for the residential neighborhoods, which flank the southern and eastern perimeters of the business district so the roots of these magnificent giants have long been burrowing their way through the lawns toward the unimposing bungalows they have shadowed for generations.

As I continue north on the avenue which is the backbone of my childhood, my gaze penetrates the front door and walls of these houses, and I see the faces of my friends as they were during my youth and hear their voices falling gently in my head.

I am startled back to reality by a loud and happy "Mister Harper, is that you?"

As I look up look up, I realize I completed my stroll in a trance and am standing in the front entrance of the drug store.

"Mister Harper, over here."

I turn my head and find myself staring into the beaming face of Naomi Waters who has worked for my family since she was sixteen years old. She nursed my mother as an infant, raised me, and continued with PK. She has been a fixture in our home for three generations. She left only after Nan and Hank were unable to keep her. Except for gray hair, she hasn't changed a whit, not one ounce lighter or one inch taller.

"I thought you had moved away from here for good. What you doing here?"

"Nomi [my childhood name for her], I'm so glad to see you! I just came home last week. How are you and what are you doing these days?"

"I'm bout the same; my rumatiz still gets me on wet and cold days. I was with Mrs. Lucie Jacobs until last week. She got so forgetful they had to put her in the rest home over in Wetumpka. Her son's there and he wanted her closer to him and his family."

"Nomi, I need somebody to help at the house. If you're interested, I'll tell you more about it on the way back home."

"You know you're my baby Mr. Harper. I'll be glad to do whatever I can. How's Miss Nan and PK?"

"Well that's what we need to talk about. Where are you heading?"

"I was going to the Piggly."

"If you have time to come home with me, we can talk about it on the way. Can you walk that far with no problem?"

"Git outta here. I could always out walk you and still can. Let's get to moving."

Thirteen

"Never on Sunday"...I Wish

Sunday has always been a special day. When Nan and I were in school, both studying and teaching, this was the day of freedom. I started Sundays with the peace and quiet of my regular activities, the paper and coffee which transitioned to writing and gallons of sweet tea, a Southern tradition even in the winter months.

When I was living here, Nan and PK followed their own schedules—most of Nan's day was spent entertaining PK to leave me in solitude. We usually changed shifts around four in the afternoon. Nan's first move was to the bathtub where she spent an hour soaking away the aches of the previous week and preparing her for the same routine in the upcoming six days.

I begin this beautiful autumn Sunday in my usual way. There's no competition for the paper since Nan and PK are still sleeping and I heard Hank go out the door for a run. I pour a cup of coffee from the pot already warming on the counter. The twelve-cup Krups is half full since Hank and I are the only admitted caffeine addicts in the house. Nan never developed a taste for it; hot chocolate was her poison. In fact, anything chocolate was her vice. Deep in her heart she has always known chocolate is a major source of caffeine, but she would never admit it.

I grab the neatly folded *Birmingham News* from the table and head to the glassed-in porch to begin my morning ritual. When I look at the front page, the words "Sunday Edition" burst off the paper like flashing headlines on a marquee to remind me this is the day of my impending ordeal, the family dinner with Queen Clairisse and her subjects. I sit in my usual chair in the corner of the porch. With my first sip of coffee comes the determination not to let this evening's nightmare ruin the rest of my day.

The three-block walk to Clairisse's house seems like the last mile of death-row.

As I approach the front door, I make a mental comparison to my last visit; nothing has changed. As usual, Nelly Belle answers the door.

"Lord, Mr. Harper. It's so good to see you. You haven't changed a bit in these last few years. You're so fat."

"Nelly Belle, I'm really happy to see you too." I couldn't help laughing at her comment. Obviously her sight was getting worse since she didn't notice my slightly graying hair around the temples. Since good health and prosperity are often indicated by plumpness in the old generation African-American culture, telling someone he or she is *fat* is a wonderful compliment. "I thought you were going to have those cataracts removed."

"I'm going to have the operation next month."

"Well good luck to you."

"Thank you, sir."

"I guess I'd better go in there now."

"They're waiting for you."

I take a deep breath and walk into the living room. They're all there. Jerry and Suzanne are sitting on the sofa along the right wall. Jerry, who is two years older than Charlene, has grayed considerably and as he stands to shake my hand, I notice he has dropped a few pounds over the past five years. His face is showing the strains of heavy drinking and many years of living under the constant criticism of an intolerant matriarch. As I take his right hand in mine, I feel the slight trembling and cool clamminess of his sweating palms. He raises his gaze and I see the black circles surrounding his eyes and emphasizing the tiny little red lines radiating from the pupils through the irises. He could play the monster in any horror movie without an ounce of makeup.

Suzanne, his wife of almost twenty years, is reminiscent of a worn-out new mother after a prolonged forty-eight hour labor to birth a ten-pound baby. Her complexion is indubitable evidence of years of neglect. Her once-blonde hair is now multicolored from the need of a long-overdue touchup. She sticks out her hand to acknowledge my arrival.

"Harper, what a pleasure. It's been too long, five years has it?" I could hear the gravel of every cigarette she has chain smoked over the years. "I've kept up with you through your books. They're very clever, you know."

"So I've been told, Suzanne. How are you?" I am hoping she ignores my question and spares me of the details.

Charlene stands to give me a big hug. "Harper, I don't think you have met my husband, the Reverend George Howell. George, this is our famous cousin, the celebrated author, Harper Wolfe."

As we exchange pleasantries, I take as close a look as I can without gawking. He looks like the typical Baptist preacher. His tiny ears are accentuated by his silver hair which is slicked back in an un-parted poof resembling an ole-time circuit gospel singer. He wears a suit and tie, that definitely looks out of place considering everyone else's casual attire. He grabs my hand with both of his huge paws in the "welcome sinner to the fold" handshake which he obviously perfected during his revival days.

"Welcome, my son. It is certainly a pleasure to meet you after hearing so many glowing reports of your success in the literary world."

The funeral tone of his voice and his overall demeanor puts a distinct uneasiness in my stomach. There is definitely something about this man that makes me want to back up to the wall and cover my balls.

"Nice to finally meet you too. George, was it?"

From the kitchen door comes the unforgettable voice of the queen herself. "Harper, we're so glad you could join us this evening. Where's PK?"

"Sorry, Clairisse. He has good days and not so good days. He's having a rough time today." I hope my lie is convincing. The truth is, I let him off the hook considering all he has been going through. I knew he'd be the only non-adult here and would be very uncomfortable under even the best of circumstances.

Clairisse turns to Jerry and says in a very sarcastic voice, "Jerry, if you can find your way to part with some of your precious scotch, why don't you offer Harper a drink?

"I would love one. Just scotch on the rocks please." I am going to need all the starch I can get to make it through what is already promising to be a long evening.

I notice the Reverend is not drinking, but Charlene has a glass of wine in tow which she raises toward me and says, "Welcome home honey. You'll find we're all the same wrecks as when you left five years ago."

"Now Charlene, Harper is going to think we're all unhappy here."

Jerry hands me a glass which is filled to the brim. "I poured you a stiff one. You'll need it to survive dinner with this ship of fools."

Clairisse snidely quips to Jerry, "I'm surprised you can spare so much. I hope you'll have enough to keep your usual binge level going until dinner is over. I don't want to have to deal with a case of the DT's between courses."

Jerry returns to his seat on the couch, as far away as possible from Clairisse and George who is giving an apparent leer of disgust at Jerry and consoling agreement toward the hand who obviously butters his toast along with everyone present in her court.

"Thank you for the drink Jerry. How have y'all been?"

"Fine."

"Are you still working at the hardware store?"

"I sure am."

"He'll probably die at the key machine," Clairisse says mockingly. "He doesn't have enough gumption to try anything else. Not that anyone but Suzanne's daddy would put up with him. I'm sure her daddy feels paying him is better than having them live on dole."

I take a large gulp of the scotch hoping the glass will magically refill itself as I try to anesthetize myself against the slaughter that is taking place. I had forgotten how caustic Clairisse has always been when talking to Jerry. I feel sorry for him, but as usual, there is nothing I can do except drink, eat and wait until the carnage is over. Thankfully, after two hours, Her Excellency dismisses us from the throne room.

Fourteen

Beware of Clairisse: Bearing Gifts or Not

On Monday afternoon, Nan is startled awake by the ringing of the phone next to her bed. She usually keeps it unplugged to avoid just this problem, but last night she was too tired to remember. As she is just coming around to awareness, she hears Naomi saying, "Yes, Miss Clairisse. I'll tell her Miss Clairisse." Only one side of the conversation is enough to send chills down her back. She can't remember when she has last seen Clairisse much less how long it has been since she called just to chat. One thing she does remember beyond the shadow of a doubt; Clairisse does nothing without a motive.

As Naomi hangs up the phone, she mumbles "I swear that woman gives me heartburn in my heels. Miss Nan, that was Miss Clairisse. She's on her way over for a visit. You want me to brush your hair before or after I give you one of them nerve pills?"

Nan sits straight up in the bed. "I'll take care of my hair. You get the drugs!" Then she adds, "Where is everybody?"

"They've all gone to the picture show. Then, they're going to stop over to the Pig 'n Whistle and get some pulled pork for supper. They know how much you like it. I made some slaw and chocolate layer cake. Here, take this, darlin'. I hear the car in the driveway. Sweet Lord, I hope this pill kicks in quick."

The unmistakable tenor of Clairisse's almost baritone drawl precedes her into the room. "Nan honey, how are you feeling today? You look great darling. I think your color is a little better today.

Where are the boys?" Clairisse takes a chair and moves it closer to the bed.

Nan sits up in the bed as Naomi fluffs a pillow and places it behind her back. "They've gone to the movies, Clairisse. Did you want to see Harper about something?"

"Good! This'll give us time to girl visit. We certainly enjoyed having Harper with us last night. Of course, we missed having you and PK. Next time, if you're feeling like it, we hope you'll join us."

"Thank you Clairisse. Harper told me all about the evening. You know peach cobbler is PK's absolute favorite. He ate the portion you sent home for breakfast this morning. Thank you so much for sending him a bowlful."

"Honey, it was my pleasure."

"How is everyone in your family?" Not that Nan cared a whit, but it wouldn't be Southern to fail to inquire.

Nan shifts her position in the bed. She doesn't know how much longer she can keep up this level of saccharine chit-chat, but musters up her best behavior. She controls her inclination to blurt out—what do you want? Spit it out! She knew Clairisse wouldn't be rushed into premature disclosure.

"My brood? They're all fine and fit, except for that girl of Jerry's. Who knows where the hell she is these days or with which piece of trash. I just hope she looks for Santa Claus somewhere else this year. You can't hide that baby of hers, especially if it snows."

"Really, I've never seen her newest baby! The next time she comes to Kellersville, you'll have to bring her over." Of course, Nan knew exactly what Clairisse was referring to.

"Oh well, that's another story. Now for the reason I've come, other than to visit with you, of course. Charlene has organized the women's auxiliary at the church and they are going to bring food for the weekends."

"That's so sweet of everybody. I hope y'all won't go to a lot of trouble on our account."

"Honey, it'll be no bother at all. We know Naomi's off on Saturdays and Sundays and we want to help so you don't have to make do with whatever the men folk whip up."

"We all really appreciate y'all thinking about us."

"Lord, times have really changed. We used to have at least one servant every day of the week. Now they've gotten so expensive that we're lucky to have one two days a week. (Nan fights the urge to roll her eyes and scream). Anyway, Charlene has planned all the weekends for three months. She is so wonderful with this kind of thing. Since unfortunately, she doesn't have any children to tend to, she has all this energy to spend working for the church and helping the needy."

Nan is not particularly fond of being referred to as "needy," but she is not unduly surprised. A tradition in South, churches and communities always rally around situations of this sort. In the case of a death, there is a run on fryers at the Piggly Wiggly and food is usually at the grieving family's house before they get home from the hospital. A network of hostesses is arranged to be at the home so there will be someone to answer the door and phone at all times. The family is never left unattended until at least a day after the funeral.

Nan knows this plan is already in place for her when the time comes. Although she is genuinely touched, she expects no less. She suppresses the obvious question in her mind; why Clairisse has come instead of Charlene who obviously set the network in motion.

"Please tell Charlene how much we sincerely appreciate the community's effort and support during this hard time. Also, thank her for organizing it." She declines to mention that there will be no funeral since Hank has already made arrangements for cremation according to her wishes. She doesn't want to bring it up at this time. No need to add fat to the fire!

Clairisse casually adds, "And another thing while I'm thinking about it. George and Charlene have offered to take PK on a weekend trip, maybe to Atlanta. They think it's important for him to get away for a few days. He can take a friend and they can go to Six

Flags Over Georgia, the Cyclorama, Stone Mountain and the new aquarium that recently opened. Y'all can use the time together to rest and relax."

"That would be so nice of them. I'll mention it to PK, but you know he's so moody these days. Sometimes, he won't even leave the house to go to the movies, as much as he loves them. That's why Harper and Hank insisted he go today." She knows PK would rather take castor oil than go anywhere with George and Charlene.

"Anyway, back to the cooking plans. Caroline Honeycutt and June Albritton are doing this weekend. I remember when Caroline first married Augustus and moved here, I guess it's been about thirty years now. She couldn't cook anything. Everybody pitched in and helped her learn, especially Pauline, her mother-in-law. Now she does right well on most things. It's the thought of course. Well, I've got to run darlin'. I'll see you later. Call me if you need anything."

Nan relaxes. She doesn't have to deal with whatever it is today. It was obviously a practice run or a reconnaissance mission. Clairisse isn't ready to reveal her intentions. No use trying to figure it out. She is still spinning her web.

Fifteen

"Hunky" Hank

I know football practice and games are monopolizing all of Hank's time, and Nan all of his thoughts. He sympathizes with PK's depression and knows that in a matter of time, the teen's life will have no stability at all. He's obviously very attached to PK but hasn't expressed his feelings about PK's staying with him in Kellersville because he isn't sure his own future is here. In addition, he doesn't want to add another element of uncertainty for PK to deal with.

Based on what Nan has told me, I'm aware she and Hank have often discussed getting out of the small-town atmosphere that is stifling them. PK is the main factor keeping them from relocating. Hank doesn't want to stay in Kellersville without Nan. Had he not met and married her, he would have moved on long ago. Although during the last three months, Hank has had many times alone to think about the future, he hasn't come to any definite plan of action or at least he hasn't shared it with anyone, including Nan.

As colleagues, but not close friends, Hank and I had known each other for several years prior to the separation. When the divorce became final, Hank started coming around. Even though I'm guessing he suspected the circumstances of the separation, he and Nan never discussed it.

They married only two years ago, as much for convenience—consolidated living expenses—as for a genuine, mutual fondness. Neither felt a burning and passionate love, but a reciprocal need.

Hank never lost awareness of Nan's life with me. Over the last two years, their bond has tightened, but Nan thinks he has never been totally free of my shadow. Now, I am a part of his life, if only temporarily. I can sense the tension between us. At times it is more obvious. I'm not really sure how we are going to feel about this after several weeks. But for now we are dealing with it fairly well.

Their arrangement appears to be well defined. Even though Hank is a math teacher, Nan covers the household, finances and other family affairs. Hank and PK share the repairs and yard chores. Gradually, PK is getting more and more involved with Hank and actually enjoying it. Hank is a good role model in spite of their diferent interests. He is an excellent math teacher and, of course, the football coach. The football coach is always a much respected figure in the community, especially when they have a winning season, a definite plus in the South.

Hank hadn't actually planned to be a football coach. He has an excellent mathematical background. His bachelor's and master's degrees were from the University of North Carolina, Chapel Hill.

Because he accepted government aid for all six years, he had to repay the loans. If he took a job in a regular school system, he would be responsible for reimbursement of half each annual payment. However, teaching in a school system designated as depressed and/or heavily minority would cancel his entire scheduled repayment for each year. In five years, he would be able to satisfy all his financial obligations. Kellersville High School was such a school. Agreeing to be an assistant coach was one of the requirements of the job. Besides, there was a coaching supplement which would come in very handy. He looked on it as a temporary situation. Then he and Nan married.

As a result of Nan's continuing disability and declining strength, I am taking over all those responsibilities for which Hank had always depended on Nan. I'm even making and packing his lunch and keeping the family checkbook as well. Hank even finds himself coming to me for his spending money. Oddly enough, we've both come to be more and more comfortable with this role. I did a little creative financial snooping and insisted Hank take the second semester off as sick leave. He has certainly accumulated enough days and his full-time efforts will be required in the final weeks of Nan's illness.

In the evenings after Nan has finally drifted off for the night and PK is in his room studying, reading or on the computer, Hank and I rest in the living room reading the paper, watching the late news and discussing the day's events concerning Nan, PK and school about which we increasingly share our feelings, emotions and fears. I have begun to look forward to the end of the day and the let-up from the growing intensity of care that Nan's rapid decline requires. Even with Naomi's help, it has become a fulltime task for two people to maintain the house and care for Nan's needs. As expected, she has both good and not-so-good days. Still the hospital is not an option—a hospice is nowhere near Kellersville. We'll just have to manage.

Sixteen

Spinning Her Web

"I had a big surprise today," Hank informs me as he sits down with his glass of wine. "When I got ready to leave the school, I went by the office and there was a message to call Clairisse. When I returned the call, she asked me to drop by on the way home. In all these years, she has never given me the time of day so I knew she was up to something. I didn't know anything else to do but go. Besides, there was only one way to find out. I wasn't in the house ten minutes until she made her offer. She wants to give us a plot in the family section of the cemetery for Nan. While I was trying to get up the courage to tell her Nan wanted to be cremated, she gave me this list of all the arrangements she had made for the funeral." He hands me the list.

As I finish reading the details of the funeral and burial services, all I can do is to sit down and shake my head in total disbelief.

"This is pushy for even Clairisse. She has selected the pallbearers from the group of deacons of the church, planned the music, the scriptures to be read, outlined the sermon for George, and planned the cars to be borrowed for the family procession."

Hank nods his head. "Yes, I know."

"What did you tell her?"

"Harper, I cut and ran. I've never dealt with her before. I didn't know what to say and I wasn't sure she was expecting me to say or do anything. All I could do was to thank her, take the paper and leave."

"You're right. She never believes anyone will have the courage to buck her and her ideas. I'll have to deal with it tomorrow before this gets even more out of hand. But for now, I need a real drink and time to think this thing out. Have you had dinner? Let's go to the Roadhouse. I could use a good steak."

"That sounds super. PK's over at Patrick Jensen's for the evening. I'll just tell Nan where we'll be if she needs us. Be back in a minute."

As Hank left the room, a brief thought of regret ran through my mind. Although we were never close friends, when we were teaching together, I had a small crush on him and occasionally even fantasized about having a tumble. I nicknamed him (to myself of course) "Hank the Hunk." He was the classic boy next door type, light brown hair, blue eyes, not too muscular but definitely well formed. Since it was obvious he wasn't aware of my admiration nor would he have been receptive if he had, I soon overcame the fantasies, but not the attraction. When Nan wrote me she and Hank were dating, I remembered experiencing a little pang of jealousy— I wasn't sure of whom.

I think I've handled this return home very well; actually it's turning out to be easier than I thought it would be as far as Nan and Hank's relationship is concerned. Now we are going out to eat alone, the opportunity I had always wished for. I can't help wondering if this is a good idea. Where will it lead? Am I just being too sensitive or reading too much into a natural situation?

As we got into Hank's pickup, I had a tingling sensation at the base of my spine, the same feeling I get every time I anticipate an encounter. This is not comforting. He is my dying ex-wife's husband. Could there be a bigger guilt trip? It is too late now. Looking at Hank, it is evident he is oblivious to the situation—thank God!

At the restaurant, we are seated at a four top which allows some breathing room. My first intention is to order a couple of martinis and drink myself into a stupor. But I bow to my better judgment and to maintain control, I take the safer option, a beer.

After we ordered our steaks, the conversation turns to the funeral and Clairisse.

"I decided to talk to Nan and find out exactly what her wishes are before I confront Clairisse. Maybe she will agree to a memorial service at a later date. Knowing what Nan wants will make it easier to put my foot down."

Hank smiles. "That's a good idea. I know what we discussed last year when we were just talking about the 'what ifs,' but I don't know if she is still adamant about it now that it is a reality."

By this time, Hank has had two beers plus the one before leaving home and only the salad has arrived. Not that he ate any of the lettuce wedge since he is strictly the meat-and-potatoes type and after scraping off the blue cheese dressing, had pushed the greens to the side.

With a little back and forth motion of his suspended beer can which was supported by his elbow on the table, he slightly lowers his eyes and drops the bomb. "You know, Nan never mentioned any of the details of your separation. I know she still loves you a lot and you obviously still have feelings for her. Although she never said anything, I sort of put two and two together."

In spite of my forte of putting situations into words, I am stunned silent. I'm reasonably sure Hank hadn't intended to shock. This opinion was immediately confirmed by the obvious look of embarrassment on his face when he realized he had verbalized his thoughts and put me on the spot.

In a split-second analysis of the situation I decide the best reply is an honest one. "Yes, I am gay. I know I really hurt Nan, but I couldn't live a double life any longer. She knew it and I knew it. She was the first to bring it up. Thank God since I'm not sure I would have had the courage to admit it to her, much less leave her and PK. She was right of course. She's a very special woman to deal with it in so mature and rational way."

"Harper, I'm so sorry I said anything. I really didn't mean for it to come out this way. I just feel it's important for us to be honest with each other. I'm comfortable with it. It's important you know you don't have to put up a guard for me. I didn't intend to ruin our first time to relax away from the house."

"You didn't ruin it. You actually made it more relaxing for me."

I wonder just how at ease he would be if he knew about the secret crush from several years ago and how much this would look like a date in other parts of the country.

Seventeen

Time to Tap Dance

The next afternoon I sit down and outline my plan for both my conversation with Nan and ultimately the "Black Widow," an appropriate name since after screwing her victim, she turns and devours all of his self-respect. I want to tell Nan in a way that won't cause her to have an anxiety attack at learning of Clairisse's audacity in making her funeral plans. This is going to be a challenge since Nan has always been able to see through most of my attempts at bull shit. As a result, I rarely tried to pull the wool over her eyes. I always seem to give everything away by the expressions on my face when I'm beating around the bush. I decide the direct approach will definitely be better in this case.

As I walk into her bedroom, I start a little ironic laugh which I use to try to soft pedal an unpalatable comment. "Just when you think Clairisse has had an epiphany and is doing something kind for a change…well, you know the story. You'll never guess what happened yesterday."

Nan sat up in the bed. "Am I going to need a Valium for this?"

"No, but you're going to need a good sense of humor."

"Well, Sweetie, I'm fresh out of that. What has she done now? Converted to Islam? Taken the veil?"

As usual Nan immediately realizes my effort and makes a light-hearted retort which gives me the opportunity to laugh heartily for the first time since I arrived in Kellersville.

"No, but it's stranger than her usual shenanigans. She called Hank at work yesterday and asked him to stop by on the way home from school."

"Oh shit. What the hell did she want?"

She wanted to offer him a spot for you in the family plot."

Her screech is a mixture of pain, disbelief and a big belly laugh. "Oh sweet Jesus, Mary, and Joseph! What did she say when he told her I was going to be cremated?"

When I don't respond, she guesses the answer. "He didn't tell her!"

"Nan, Hank hasn't had the years of experience dealing with Clairisse like the rest of us. He was overwhelmed and dumbstruck. I actually felt sorry for him when he related the story. He said he did all he could to muster up the guts to tell her, but in the end, he was intimidated and left."

"You're right, of course. We've all been there before. This was his first time face to face with the enemy in battle. Bless his heart, was he shaking and scarred for life?"

"He did the best he could."

"I know. I don't blame him. She is formidable! God, what nerve this woman has! What business is it of hers?"

"Hon, you know that has never been one of her worries." I say to interject more support for Hank's vulnerability.

"The bitch won't even let me die on my own terms. I didn't live to please her, and I'm damn sure not going to die to her specifications. The next thing you know, she'll be planning a blow-out funeral."

I'm certain she is just ranting and accidentally hit the bull's eye, but I take this opportunistic opening to spring the rest on her.

"Funny you should mention it! Here's the list." I hand her Clairisse's two page outline of the funeral arrangements.

Nan is speechless. She sits for a few moments before looking at the paper. Then she starts to laugh. "Well, I'll have to give her credit. She's branching out. She's finally gotten tired of the everyday grind of stage-managing the people around her and has expanded her talents to controlling folks beyond the grave. Will you take care of her or do I have to? I've got nothing to lose. Just bring her on!"

"Alright, calm down. You know I'll tell her. But first, I need to know what *you* want. Do you have anything written down? Any instructions for the final hurrah?"

"No. But I will sure as hell tell you what I *don't* want. I am not having all those old women hanging over my casket saying 'Don't she look natural? She looks like she's just sleeping. They did such a good job on her you'd hardly know she was dead.' And I don't want to go near the Lord's Holy Free Will Calvary Baptist Church—either the First or the Second. I've avoided it all my life. Death will not change a thing."

Then she pauses for a brief but pensive moment. "Alright Leroy, spit it out." She never calls by my middle name unless she suspects I'm holding something back and she is trying to pin me down. She, of course, emphasized the first syllable for the express purpose of pissing me off enough to drop my guard.

"I agree with everything you've just said. I just know Kellersville and Southern 'funeralizing.' You know the event is more for the survivors than the departed. It gives closure. It's a social affair and everyone looks forward to the opportunity to grieve with their friends and neighbors. Nowadays, people have memorial services even weeks after the death. I just hope you'll agree to a little get together. Maybe this will shut Clairisse up."

"I knew there was something else. You planned your strategy well. I walked right into your trap. You think I ought to do it."

"Yes, I do."

"Are you sure you're not holding back something else?"

"What more could there be?"

"I don't know, but when Clairisse is involved, the surprises never seem to end."

"That's all. I promise."

"Okay. But here are the conditions. No church! No preacher! No flowers! And definitely no old biddy singing hymns. Do it any other way and I'll haunt you so hard you'll wish Clairisse had your balls on a short rope."

"Agreed!" Now all I have to do is deal with Clairisse.

Eighteen

Wheeling and Dealing With the Master Dealer

I grab the door jamb to support my shaking legs and bite my lip to fight the urge to scream in horror when Clairisse answers the door clad in a bright-yellow smock with thin black oriental figures embroidered on the left breast which are probably supposed to be her initials. Combined with her newly-dyed reddish-brown hair, it makes her look like a giant summer squash on the verge of going bad.

"Thank you so much for taking the time out of your schedule to let me drop by for a little chat. I hope I didn't interrupt anything." I follow her through the living room and a seat on the glassed-in sun porch where Clairisse has placed the fixings for a cup of coffee and shortbread biscuits.

As she is pouring the coffee she asks "What do you take in it?"

"Just a little cream, no sugar please."

She puts in the cream, stirs it twice, hands me the cup and a small napkin, and gestures to the cookies on the coffee table in front of me.

As she is pouring herself a cup, I decide to open the conversation. "You were so kind and thoughtful to offer Hank a spot in the family plot for Nan. It really makes her feel she is still a part of the family."

"Well of course she is sweetie. She's still PK's mother and very dear to us all. We wouldn't think of having her buried anywhere else. I know she's an orphan and doesn't have a family plot of her own."

"I can't tell you how humbled she is at the kind offer, but the fact is, Nan wants to be cremated."

The visible effects of my pronouncement are the highest degree of shock I have ever experienced on Clairisse's face. Her hands begin to shake so badly that she almost spills the coffee on the rug. She is clearly disoriented by the revelation. She appears to start to speak, but no sound emerges from her lips.

"Are you alright?" I say as I take the cup from her trembling hand.

When she finally finds the breath to support her words, she babbles in a rapid disorientated stream accompanied by a wild flaying of her left hand. Her right hand remains noticeably still.

"Cremated? Cremated?" Her words start erupting like lava from Etna. "I've never known anyone who has been cremated. No one in Kellersville has ever been cremated and certainly not in *our* family. Where in the hell did she get such an idea? Why, I don't even know anybody in…in… all of Randolph County who's ever been *cremated.* It's so… so… un-Baptist!"

"Try to calm down. This is really quite common these days." I am patting her on the shoulder in a vain effort to reduce her anxiety.

"It may be common somewhere else, but not in Kellersville."

"I was just saying…"

"You're right. It *is* common; common as collards. I just can't imagine it." She unconsciously grabs her right arm with her left hand. "Oh sweet Mary, Mother of God. This can't be happening to me. I just don't believe I can face people and say Nan is being …*cremated!*"

"Actually it's…"

"What about the *funeral*? What will people say? Everybody will think we can't afford to give her a decent burial. And we're in the funeral business, for God's Sweet Sake. What kind of advertisement is that? First thing you know, everybody will get the same idea and where will we be? Out of business, for sure. Of course, it's cheaper to just *throw 'em* on the bar-b-cue pit and be done with it!" She wildly waves her hand in an outward and upward motion as if shooing away a fly.

When she stops for a breath, I take the opportunity to break in. "Nan is very firm on this. Afterwards, we'll have a nice memorial service so everyone can pay their respects. I think this compromise will please Nan."

"A memorial service? What the hell is a *memorial service*? I have never even *heard* of such, much less *been* to one." She clasps her right hand over her forehead. "I'm a Baptist, for God's sake, a member of the Junior League of Kellersville and *everything else* that's important. I have *absolutely* no idea how to plan a *me-mo'-ri-al* service."

"I have written down the main points that Nan has requested. You can fill in the rest. Hank and I'll be glad to help, but we'll be depending on you. Here is the outline for the service. On these points, Nan is firm."

When I give her the list, she looks long and hard at the details written on the small piece of blue stationary Nan always uses for her personal notes. Not that she ever considered writing a personal note to Clairisse, but under the circumstances, she doesn't see any need in saving the embossed note paper for later occasions.

1. Place: funeral home or high school auditorium
2. Speaker: Matthew Parks, Principal of Kellersville High School
3. Music: Ruth Ginsberg, music teacher at the high school
4. In lieu of flowers, contributions to the Kellersville High School Library
5. No prayers or hymns

She finishes reading the list and pauses for a deep breath. Shaking her head in disbelief she finally speaks. "She's very definite, I'll say that much. Well at least this gives me an idea of what she wants. I can guarantee you this will be a first in Kellersville. I hope they don't take offense to this idea. They might feel slighted at not having a body to ogle."

"Thank you again for the kind offer of the burial plot. Nan will be so happy you're not offended that she is declining." I rise to leave. Out of some crazy and incontrollable instinct, I bend down and peck her on the cheek. When I realize what I have done, I make a bee line for the front door to quickly exit so as not to reveal the scarlet flush that is flowing upward to my forehead and burning my cheeks to the point of perspiration.

Upon reaching home, I relate the entire scenario to Nan, except the errant display of affection, of course, which I intend never to reveal to anyone.

Nineteen

Confession: Good for the Soul?

PK was waiting for Hank to pick him up at the school after play practice. PK never had any desire to be on the stage; acting wasn't real enough for him. He had gotten interested in the mechanics of the support faction when the new computerized lighting and sound system arrived at Kellersville High last year. His curiosity drew him into the drama department and he had been hooked ever since.

When I called him on the cell phone to let him know I was coming to pick him up instead of Hank, he said it had just started to rain. As he gets into the car, I hand him a towel and a change of shirt.

"How'd it go at practice?" I said as I turned out of the circular driveway in front of the school.

"Great. We're getting better. At least everybody knew all their lines this afternoon. Why the clean shirt? Have we got company?"

"No. I'm taking you to the Paulo's Pizza Palace. Hank and Nan need some time alone. I made them a chicken dinner and all they have to do is warm it in the microwave."

PK laughed. "That's good because microwaving is Hank's limit. That and cereal."

As we pull into the parking lot of the restaurant, I take a final breath to brace myself for the discussion I know is long overdue. Although the restaurant is almost empty, I walk directly toward a table in the back corner so we can have privacy. After we put in our order, I decide to postpone it no longer.

"Son, it's time we had a very important talk, just the two of us."

PK sifts uneasily in his chair and raises his glance to meet mine. "If this is the *birds and bees* spiel, Hank has already filled me in on the things I didn't already know from the other guys."

"No, that's not it. Maybe sometime we can compare notes and you can fill me in on what I'm missing. But for now, we need to cover another base."

"Mom?"

"PK, this is a big time in your life. Most people live to a nice old age before they lose a parent. Trust me, it's not easy at any age, but it's harder at your age when you haven't had nearly enough time with them."

I notice tears beginning to well up in his eyes and for an instant I question my timing. Then I realize I can't prolong it.

"You've had to grow up a lot in these few months and you are handling it so well. I wish we had had this conversation before now when everything seems to be falling apart for us all. But the fact is, we didn't. I thought we had a lot of time to deal with it. Now, I am going to have to put something else on your plate."

The waitress momentarily interrupts me as she leans over the table to serve our two cokes.

"Your mother and I grew up together from kindergarten. We love each other so much, even now. But there are times when things change; change so much that we can't go on any longer without altering our lives. Nan didn't change, I did. Well, I didn't actually change so much as I decided I had to take a different road in life. Your mother is the only woman I have ever loved other than my mother of course. I just couldn't continue to live as her husband because it wasn't fair to her. I realized I was sexually attracted to other men. I had to make a decision. I thought it was better to let you two get on with your lives without me. We divorced, but we never grew apart; even when she married Hank."

He looks up to see PK's reaction. The tears have disappeared and he isn't registering any emotion on his face. I have no outward sign as to his degree of comprehension of what I am telling him.

Maybe growing up in Kellersville has sheltered him so that he doesn't understand; I was hoping I wouldn't have to draw a picture.

"I know this is probably very difficult for you to comprehend and deal with because you live in Kellersville. Someday you'll understand. As I said before, I'd hoped we would have a few more years until we had to deal with it, but now you and I will be living together and you have to know the truth. We can't have a life together without total honesty."

PK put his hand on my arm. "I thought that was it. I mean, I really didn't know for sure, but I figured it out. You're not like my friends' fathers. You talk about different things and act smarter than they do. Besides, you're a famous writer. I Googled you last year and one of the articles said you were probably gay. It's no big deal to me. You're still the greatest."

Now tears swell in my eyes and the lump in my throat prevents an immediate response.

The pizzas arrive just in time. The rest of the meal is easier than I could have imagined. We make small talk while we eat and I feel a huge relief from the biggest burden I have shouldered since Nan and I had our heart-to-heart talk five years ago.

By the time we get home, everything seems normal. Nan is asleep. Hank is drinking a beer in the living room. I pour myself a glass of wine and sit in the easy chair near the sofa.

"How did it go? What was his reaction?"

"How did you know?"

"I knew it was time."

"It went better than I could have hoped."

In the darkness of his bedroom, PK cries himself to sleep. Not because his father is gay, but because one of his biggest fears has been allayed; his father loves him and wants him.

Twenty

Roll Tide!

From the living room where I am working on the draft for my next mystery, I hear the kitchen door slam and look up to see Hank almost skipping into the house. As he sees Naomi in the kitchen, he runs over and gives her a big hug.

She looks at him and laughs. "Child, I don't know what you're expecting for supper, but we ain't having pot roast 'til *tomorrow* night."

"That's not it. But I'll look forward to tomorrow night for sure. Your pot roast is worth waiting for. Of course, it goes better with your famous banana pudding bringing up the rear." Hank hopes she will take the hint. Obviously, he hit the right spot to flatter her.

"Lord child, you won't do! What's got the yeller jacket in your britches?"

"Jim Braxton just gave me two Alabama/Auburn tickets! He can't go because his mother-in-law died, and he has to go to St. Louis for the funeral. At first, he considered going to the game instead of the funeral, but he knew he might as well just pack his clothes on the way out the door. Poor guy, it was a hard decision to have to make."

Nan sticks her head around the door. "It's absolutely selfish of that old lady to die at such an inconsiderate time. The least they could do is hold her out for a few extra days."

Of course, Nan says this in jest. But the truth of the matter is there's no way any self-respecting Alabama resident would even die during this time, and if they did, no one would attend the funeral if it were held on the Saturday of this sacred weekend. Everybody in the South, especially Alabama, knows football. It is a part of life from infancy. Pink and blue baby clothes are out of the question during pigskin season; they are thrown aside in favor of apparel sporting Tide or Tiger logos. Allegiances are determined before walking or talking—there's no other way. In Alabama, the only mixed marriage that is barely considered acceptable is one where there's one spouse from Alabama and the other from Auburn; and this takes a special dispensation from family and close friends.

When Hank moved into the state, the principal told him, "You have to pick a team. It doesn't make any difference where you went to school before you got here. It's either the Tide or the Tigers—you've got to pull for one or the other."

Everybody knows the sky's the limit when considering what people of both sides will wear this week: elephant or tiger purses, shirts, hats, jackets, shoes, socks, belts, trousers, skirts and even underwear, a sight that even the most conservative belle will gladly share after the game if her team wins.

"Naomi, will you see if you can find Hank's Tide paraphernalia?"

"His what?"

Nan laughed. "All his clothes and things with Bama and Tide on them."

"Even those underpants with the elephants on 'em in the back of his drawer?"

"That's ok." Hank blushes and turns toward Nan.

Nan continues "Hank, who're you going to take with you? PK has already left for the three-day computer camp in Atlanta. I think this would be a great opportunity for you and Harper to become better acquainted. When we were at the University, we went to all the games. He used to be a big fan."

"That'd be great, but since the game starts at six and won't be over until at least ten, driving back would be impossible. Because of this, Jim and Helen have reservations for the night."

Nan breaks in. "So what's the problem? I'm sure y'all can take that room and reimburse Jim and Helen. The motel won't care so long as they get their money."

"One of us needs to be here to spend the night with you."

Naomi breaks in "I can stay overnight. That way, you both can go. I'll fry some chicken and pack y'all some pimento-cheese sandwiches and stuffed eggs. I'll have the pot roast ready to heat up for Sunday night's supper."

"That'll be super if it's alright with Nan." Hank adds.

"Of course it's alright with me. I'll be fine. Y'all go on and bring back a Bama win!"

My second thought is to find some excuse and decline, but I crumble and go with my first temptation and accept. It's not that I've completely lost interest in football; I've picked up a new interest—Hank. For this reason, I'm not at all sure it's a good idea to go off with him for the night, but I'm certain I can handle the tricky situation, especially since I'm totally convinced Hank doesn't suspect my feelings. Nan obviously has no reservations since she is eagerly encouraging the idea. It will be a great opportunity to get out of Kellersville for a needed respite.

Although until recent years, the annual cross-state rivalry was a perennial event at Legion Field in Birmingham, the game now alternates between Tuscaloosa and Auburn on a yearly basis. The trip to Tuscaloosa is very pleasant. We talk only briefly about Nan and her situation. The conversation mainly centers on PK and how he will handle his relocation to California and my plans for his education. After a few limp attempts to discuss the current Tide team and season, the subject eventually comes around to Hank's plans for the future.

"I don't know what I'm going to do. I definitely will take the second semester to fill out some applications and go on some interviews. I really don't want to stay here if I don't have to. I just have no idea where I'll apply. I'd like to get out of Alabama. If they are as short of math teachers as everybody says, I should have no problems getting some interesting interviews and maybe a few good offers."

When we get to the motel, we are faced with the first hurdle. The woman at the reservation desk informs us all rooms with two beds have been rented; the reservation the Braxtons have is for a king and that is all that is left. She offers to put a cot in the room for no extra charge if there is one left. Since we obviously have no alternative, we decide to make the best of it; after all it is a *king* size.

When we arrive at the The University, there is no parking left in the lot surrounding Bryant-Denny Stadium although we are relatively early. We are flagged into the make-shift parking lot in front of one of the apartment complexes that pepper the campus around the stadium. Parking is ten bucks. Two of the apartments have been designated as restrooms at an additional charge of two dollars a visit or an all-day pass for five. Student ingenuity has certainly changed since the Denny Chimes, the landmark campus time keeper, last rang in my ears.

"You know all this dust has made me very thirsty," said Hank. "What say we have a couple of beers before we break out Naomi's wonderful supper."

I glance around. The cars are jammed bumper-to-bumper. This not only maximizes profits, it puts everyone so close there are really no individual groups. It's just one huge party of people who will be best friends for one brief and hopefully memorable evening. Everything about the tailgating and the game is the same as I remember. It brings back so many wonderful memories of the four years Nan and I spent at the University. We had our whole life ahead of us. The biggest hurdle at that time was deciding whether or not to go back to Kellersville to teach or look for another school together. Neither of us ever imagined we would ever be in this situation.

As we are sipping the suds, I hear my name called from two cars over to the right. The voice sounds familiar but I can't put it with a face. Then I catch sight of Paul Steiner.

"Harper, what are you doing here, in Alabama, I mean."

"I'm here on a family visit. [Harper noticed Paul's quizzing glance toward Hank.] This is Hank Warner, my ex-wife's husband. He had an extra ticket and since this is my Alma Mater, well… here I am."

"I wanted to call you, but the airlines lost the bag with your phone number and address. I tried Directory Assistance in Palm Springs, but you have an unlisted number. Last month, I sent you a letter in care of your publisher, no reply."

"I've been in Alabama for over a month."

"I thought you didn't ever want to return home."

"I didn't and don't. There are complications." Over the next hour, I give Paul a brief account of the past few months.

"It appears you certainly have your plate full. I'm really sorry you had to come back under the circumstances, but at least we've reconnected."

"That's a definite plus, but the only one I can see. Where are you living now? Why are you here?"

"I got a fantastic offer to teach for the Law School at Emory. It has given me an opportunity to make some contacts in the South and look for a firm to join. I've had several interesting avenues to explore, but I haven't made a commitment to anything yet. I'm actually here on an interview. Everyone in the firm is a graduate of The University, so I was brought here as a baptism into the regional religion."

"I see they taught you how to piss off the 'Auburnites' by saying *The University*."

He laughs. "It was the first thing I learned."

We spend the rest of the pre-game social activities visiting with everyone in their respective groups. I agree to come to Atlanta for a few days of R & R at the first of December. If Paul takes the job in Birmingham, it won't start until January 1.

The Tide runs over the Tigers which pleases Hank and me immensely. The end of the game proves the traffic situation has not gotten any better over the years. It takes almost an hour and a half to get to the motel.

"There's no cot in the room." I say and reach for the phone. "I'll call the office and check on it."

"Good idea. But if she doesn't have an extra one, we'll make do."

After we both shower, we sit at the little table for a few minutes and watch the news, which of course, includes the highlights of the Tide's massacre of the War Eagles. Hank appears to be unshaken about the sleeping arrangements. I can't help being a bit more nervous.

Hank walks toward the bed, "Which side of the bed do you want, right or left."

"Either is fine for me. You pick." was the reply.

I spend the night hanging onto the edge of the bed in a desperate attempt to avoid any contact during the night. Although I am successful, I don't get much sleep. After a good breakfast in the motel restaurant, we head back to Kellersville. In spite of my apprehensions about the trip, it went quite well. I feel as if I know Hank much better because of it.

Everyone at home is fine. The pot roast is fantastic.

Twenty-One

Paul

Paul came into my life last April. I met PK at the airport in Atlanta to start what had become a father and son tradition each spring since the divorce five years ago. Nan had put PK on the plane in Montgomery for the short flight to the capitol of the neighboring state. We were planning to spend a week at a horse ranch in the mountains just north of the Georgia-Tennessee line. We both liked to ride and had spent a week at ranches in Colorado and Wyoming on two of our previous April vacations. I had been looking forward to this week and was delighted the weather was reported to be perfect for outdoor activities.

The drive was uneventful. PK and I talked about the usual things fathers and sons discuss to establish common grounds in the first few hours of being together on these occasional custody vacations: school, friends, and events during the hiatus.

PK found an ad for this resort in a copy of *Southern Living,* which has arrived in our home every month for as long as I can remember. We had no problem following the directions to The Homestead, a little more than two hours from the airport in College Park, a southern suburb of Atlanta. The ranch was nestled in the mountains near Pidgeon Forge, the wide spot in the road which mushroomed with the opening of *Dollywood USA*, the country-music theme park owned by Miss Parton herself.

As we drove through the split-railed gate, the view was exactly what we expected from the pictures in the brochure. We were very pleased with our initial impression of the ranch and anticipated a wonderful fun-filled week together.

Our charming cabin was small with only one bedroom and one bath, a living room and a kitchen. Since the noon and night meals were prepared and served in the main chow hall, we had brought only breakfast foods: our favorite cereals, juice and coffee.

The jewel in the crown, the wonderful screened porch, which practically hung over the lively stream running through the property, was enhanced by a double-sided fireplace so that both the warmth and the ambiance could be enjoyed from the living room as well as the porch.

"PK, this is just great! You've certainly scored an ace on this place. As usual, I brought along several things I want to read. I'm really looking forward to spending some of this week relaxing with a good book out here on this wonderful porch."

As PK went out the door, he announced over his shoulder, "It's super. I think I'll go out and have a look around to see if everything else makes the grade."

The next morning, I awoke early. The air was cool and crisp so I stirred the smoldering embers from last night's fire and added two new logs. As the sleeping fireplace slowly began to flame with new life, I carried my coffee to the little table in front of the hearth on the porch to enjoy watching the leaves and twigs floating down the stream toward the road where they disappeared under the bridge to unseen and only imagined destinations.

The sounds of the morning echoed through the misty clouds hovering over the valley giving credence to the legendary appellation Great Smokey Mountains. The fragrance of perking coffee and frying bacon wafted anonymously from a neighboring cabin creating an anticipated disappointment of the cereal that awaited the first indications of emptiness.

I sat almost hypnotized by the brook's trickling sounds, which seemed to be melodically accompanying the water's lazy amble in the spring morning's sun. In this relaxing atmosphere, my mind started to recount the events of the last four years as if it were someone else's story and all I had to do was watch as it unfolded with no obligation for action nor decision. It was actually the first time since I made the fateful decision to leave Kellersville that I felt pressure to move neither physically nor mentally. It was a gigantic symbolic breath. My reverie was interrupted by PK, who emerged from the cabin.

"The orientation session will begin in thirty minutes. When I went out exploring last night, I noticed that all four cabins were well lighted. I guess that means everybody's here."

"Great. Now we can meet our fellow horse enthusiasts we'll spend the next six days with. Let's grab our cereal and get dressed."

"Oh, I'm already dressed and I ate ten minutes ago."

"I'm not quite that fast. You'll have to hold your horses or go on without me, young man."

Upon entering the main lodge, we realized we were the last to arrive. The other three families consisted of a thirty-something couple with a teenage boy who looked to be about PK's age, two sisters in the twenty-five to thirty range, and a handsome dark-haired guy with two slightly stocky girls, around ten and twelve by the looks of them. He stepped forward, extended his hand and introduced himself immediately.

"Hello! I'm Paul Steiner and these are my two daughters, Rachel and Ruth. They are still living in Philadelphia with their mother."

When I was finally able to wrench my eyes from this sexy man who had just unexpectedly walked into what I was anticipating to be an ordinary week with PK, I returned the big bright smile and grasped his firm hand. "Happy to meet you all. This is my son, PK. We just drove up last night from Atlanta."

Maybe I was reading too much into this first encounter, but I was convinced there was a spark of something between Paul and me. Whether it was reality or overly eager anticipation, I began to react to the warmth that rushed over me and the keen sense of awareness that my body was responding to his very presence.

"Would everyone please gather over here so we can start getting acquainted with our fellow riding enthusiasts?" The voice of the

Director provided a relief to the emotions that were developing almost too quickly for a father-son week.

We spent the rest of the day becoming acclimated to the ranch and its physical plant, the horses we will be riding for the next six days, and the rules, regulations and helpful hints for getting the most out of the vacation.

Because I hadn't ridden since our last vacation, the activities of the day, although limited to the immediate neighborhood, wreaked their toll on my rear end, and I looked forward to sitting on the porch after dinner with a glass of wine and the novel I started on the plane.

When we arrived at the cabin after dinner, PK announces, "They're showing a great movie in the lodge. I think it's one of the Harry Potter films."

"No thanks. You go along without me. I just want to soak my rear in a tub of hot water and relax in front of the fire."

The warmth of the water relaxed me and began to weave its spell. After I put on my favorite exercise togs and returned to the porch, I poked the fire which was started by one of the staff and was just beginning to reach the ember stage. A chaise lounge invited me to its comfortable embrace. I settled in for the evening.

After just a few minutes, Paul turned the corner with a bottle of wine and two glasses. Remembering the glint in Paul's eyes when we were introduced and the frequent smiling glances throughout the day, I found renewed energy to invite him in.

As we sat chatting and sipping the wine by the firelight, I realized that Paul Steiner was more than the average handsome man; he was a good conversationalist. Although I certainly didn't want to pry and ask personal questions of a new acquaintance, I was trying to find a way to easily know more about him without being obvious. I decided to start with a noncommittal question.

"So Mr. Steiner, what gainful employment supports your obviously comfortable lifestyle?" I secretly hold my breath and hope I haven't offended him.

"Actually, I'm an attorney. I'm divorced with two daughters who still live in Philadelphia with their mother. After finally coming to grips with my sexual orientation and realizing my inability to maintain a dual lifestyle, I asked my wife for a divorce, left my practice in Philadelphia, and moved to Atlanta to join a law firm. I also teach a class at the Emory University School of Law. I was thirty-six on my last birthday, only two weeks ago. This trip, by the way, is my birthday present to me and a way to spend the vacation time with my two daughters."

As he related his history, I observed him. His physical appearance was certainly no drawback: dark-brown to black hair and green eyes framed his flawless smile. Since Emory has one of the premier dental schools in the South, I was sure they have been professionally whitened, if not capped.

"What about you? It's your turn. I certainly know who you are. I've read your books, but the blurbs on the dust jackets don't give much information."

"My ex-wife, Nan, still lives in Kellersville, Alabama where we grew up. We divorced four and a half years ago when I finally came to grips with being gay. We haven't told PK the details of our separation."

"Has he indicated any suspicion?"

"Not at all. As far as I know, he is totally unaware. How about your girls?"

"They know. The divorce wasn't quiet."

"Sorry!"

"I'm not. I'd prefer not to have had it so out in front, but I don't have to beat around the bush. I'm sure they don't realize the full extent of the situation, and that's okay for now."

"Nan remarried a few months ago. PK seems to accept it. From what I can tell, he likes her new husband."

Our conversation continued effortlessly through the entire bottle of Pinot Grigio. It turned out the body wasn't the only thing well developed. I couldn't remember the last time I had engaged in so interesting a conversation with a guy who appealed to me sexually. The only question in my mind was what Paul was seeking out of this friendship, sex or a stimulating conversation to while away the evening; both would have been a gift from heaven and completely unexpected based on past experience.

The evening was a wonderful experience.

The next few days were right out of the brochure: wonderful days riding and exploring the terrain, excellent food and good company. By the third day, everyone had eased into the routine.

On Friday, the last full day, the director had planned an all-day trip for only the kids thereby giving the adults a day on our own. Right after breakfast, Paul came to our cabin.

"Well we're free for the next eight hours. Do you have any plans for the day?"

"What do you suggest?"

"How about a drive through the mountains and lunch anywhere but the ranch dining hall?"

"Let me get my sunglasses and cell phone." I hoped my excitement hasn't been too obvious in accepting the invitation. Playing hard to get was neither my style nor an option here since time was limited.

I don't think I was so excited about anyone since I left Kellersville and relocated to Palm Springs, by way of New York and San Francisco. As I headed toward the car, I had a foretelling feeling of an important change in my life.

The scenery along the drive through the mountains was wonderful. Invigorating conversation revealed we were of one mind on politics and the important aspects of literature, music and the Arts in general. We found a little café off the tourist-trodden main street of Gatlinburg for a delightful two-hour lunch. I really don't remember what I ate; the food was the least memorable part of the event. I truly couldn't say what stimulated me more, Paul's mind or his body.

When we arrived back at the ranch, two hours remained before the scheduled return of the excursion. Paul suggested we stop by his cabin for the end to a perfect day. I had never acted on any sexual opportunities during my visitation periods with PK. My first impulse was to continue the practice of self-imposed temporary abstinence and decline; I knew that was the right thing to do, but the right thing wasn't in control here.

Saturday morning was devoted to the preparations for departure. Though there was a scheduled gathering for the appropriate adieus, Paul and his daughters were absent because the girls had an unusually early flight from Knoxville, the nearest major airport to the ranch. While not unexpected, we had exchanged contact information last night, I was disappointed. In the perfect world of romanticism, Paul would have rescheduled his reservations and been there for an emotional goodbye scene filled with promises of undying love and devotion. Instead, all that remained were questions. Did we share the same feelings? Where would this lead? Would we ever meet again? Could I trust my emotions? Was this the beginning of the first meaningful relationship since Nan and I separated or was it just another one-night stand to be stashed away and forgotten like the others and occasionally remembered as a spring fling?

It would appear to have been a fling since I hadn't heard anything from Paul since April. The next time I saw him he had shown up at the last place I would have ever expected, an Alabama football game on a cool November afternoon.

Twenty-Two

Merry Christmas

The day after Thanksgiving, I drive to Atlanta for a three-day weekend with Paul. The two-hour drive is uneventful and presents me with lots of thinking time. We plan to spend the majority of the time relaxing, shopping and generally getting to know the finer points of each other's life. This is the first opportunity to be together since the week at the ranch.

Paul makes reservations at two excellent restaurants for Friday and Sunday nights. We are not disappointed. Both of us love good food and an interesting dining experience. The crowning highlight of the weekend is the Atlanta Opera's performance of Verdi's *Rigoletto*. Our relationship seems to be budding: good food, good music, good conversation and fantastic sex. What more can I ask for? And why do I feel something was missing?

On Monday, I set out for my return to Kellersville and what is supposed to be a holiday season of parties and family get-togethers. I want to really go all out to make this as memorable a month as possible.

I park the car, take my luggage from the trunk and enter the kitchen through the back door to find Nan and Hank sitting at the dinette table.

"You two look like there's a problem. What's up?" I put down my bags and take a seat.

Nan is the first to speak. "Since the school has three weeks vacation for Christmas, Hank promised PK they would rent an RV and take a trip for the first five or six days. Of course, this is before I threw a wrench in the works. In all the confusion, we both apparently forgot about the intended excursion. PK hasn't said a word about it, so we're not sure he remembers either."

"I'm afraid he hasn't. He always makes such detailed arrangements. I'm sure he has it all planned out."

"I knew you were going to say that. Harper, why don't you take him on the trip? I'll stay here with Nan."

"Really Hank, you ought to go and let me stay behind. The two of you have planned this time together and should go on. I'll be here. No problem!"

"Actually guys," Nan speaks up, "both of you need to go. I'm in a respite period and I have Naomi. She can stay here for the short time y'all will be gone."

Both Hank and I simultaneously begin to protest.

"Enough! I've made up your minds!"

I've been away for five years, but I still remember that tone in her voice and know the argument is over.

Obviously, Hank also realizes the futility in further dissention. "I'll call the RV place tomorrow.

All of PK's arrangements fulfills his promise to provide the elements for a fabulous extended weekend. The Biltmore, Vanderbilt's mansion in Asheville, North Carolina is more elaborate than any of us expected; it is especially spectacular all decorated for the Christmas season.

Other than the mansion, Asheville is a disappointment. Although in the summer, the Smokey Mountain range is a veritable wonderland for recreation, winter offerings fitting our lifestyles and preferences are relatively scarce. None of us are interested in skiing. A family vote results in our leaving a day early to head to Highlands, a getaway mountain community for the uppity-and-coming middle-aged professionals who make the four-hour pilgrimage from Atlanta every Friday after work.

On the first (and last) full day in Asheville, my cell phone brings a surprise. When I answer, I am both excited and anxious. The voice that responds to my greeting is instantly recognizable.

"Hi good looking. How's my best guy?" It's the first time I've heard from Paul since the trip to Atlanta a few weeks ago. There are two messages, which obviously resulted from calls received when we were in the mountains or other areas of no reception. I returned both calls and left messages, but this is our first actual person-to-person contact.

"Well finally we speak. What's going on in Hotlanta?" I asked offhandedly.

"How's the trip going? Are you guys having just a fantastic time?"

"The Biltmore is absolutely fabulous. It is all we expected and more. There's nothing else interesting in Asheville. Thomas Wolfe's house is nice, but it doesn't take much time to go through it. We're talking about leaving tomorrow and going to the Highlands-Cashiers area early."

"That's the reason I called. I'm missing you really badly. I've taken a couple of days off and thought I might drive up for a quick visit. I checked the High Hampton Inn in Cashiers and they are holding reservations until I call back to confirm. Do you want some company?"

I know I have only seconds to respond. Any delay in responding will make it sound as if Paul is intruding. "That sounds fantastic! When are you coming?

"I'll be there tomorrow. I'll call you when I get there and we'll make arrangements to meet. I'm really anxious to see you. I've got something really important to ask you. See you then."

When I hang up, I turn to the other two. I start to speak but am interrupted by PK.

"What was that all about?"

"That was Paul. He has a couple of days off and is coming to Cashiers to join us for short while

"Aw **shit!** What makes him think he'll be welcome? This is our vacation and my plans damn sure don't include **him**!"

This reaction is so un-PK it takes both Hank and me by surprise. Neither could speak for a moment. Then Hank speaks up. "Are you sure that's fair to your dad?

"Fair? You're darned right it's not fair. It's not fair for him to barge in on us during our time together. I don't want him here." Then PK realizes he has said too much. "Dad, I'm so sorry. I promised myself I wouldn't say anything about it. I wouldn't hurt you for anything. I was just so surprised. I'm really sorry." He comes over and gives me a big hug.

"PK, everyone has the right to express his opinion. I suspected you didn't care much for him, but I'm sorry it had to come out like this. Paul is very fond of you and thinks you are just slow to come around, especially since there was only that one week last spring. He's hoping you'll eventually learn to like him. I hope you will be open to his friendship. Give him a chance. I'm sure he's coming here to spend more quality time with you as well as to see me."

All through this exchange, Hank is very quiet. I can tell by the expression on his face, he agrees with me that PK should give Paul a fair shake, but I sense he also thinks this may be too much too fast for the teenager to digest. Since there is no way he can enter this debate, he obviously decides to take a powder.

"I want to check the tires on this baby before we start out. I'll be back in a minute."

I reach over and touch him on the arm. "This concerns all of us. Please don't leave."

Hank tries to lighten up the situation. "I don't know why he's coming, but I'm reasonably sure it's not to see **me**!" The three of us laugh and everything seems to calm down; for the time being anyway.

When we arrive in Cashiers, Paul is waiting at the lodge. Everyone has agreed to make the best of what is obviously an uncomfortable situation.

Hank speaks out as we drive through the gates of the High Hampton Inn, an historic country-mountain inn with the reputation of snootiness in keeping with the arbitrary elitism which runs through the fresh mountain air in Cashiers, North Carolina. The custom of requiring coats and ties for dinner seems incongruous with accommodations in a rustic log cabin, at not so rural prices.

"Alright guys, we are very aware of the ticklish diplomacy that is going to be needed in the next two days to avoid embarrassing Paul beyond belief. None of us would want to be in his situation and realize he is so unwanted and unwelcome by any of us. Therefore, we are going prove ourselves the gracious Southern gentlemen our mothers all raised us to be. We are going to go all out in an effort to make him have a good time." Hank looks directly at PK. "Are we all in agreement? PK?"

PK nods. "I'll be 'Parker Perfect', don't worry."

I reach over and put my hand on Hank's shoulder. "Thank you Hank. Nan would be proud!"

Paul comes and goes without mentioning the important question he was planning to ask me. This is the only indication that he had even the tiniest suspicion he may not have been the most welcome of additions to our party.

Twenty-Three

Deck the Halls

Kellersville takes Christmas very seriously. Everyone decks out in the finest yuletide tinsel and lights: stores, houses, offices and streets. There is always a parade the first Saturday of December to usher Santa Claus to town. The majority of the floats are pick-up trucks decorated in the most elaborate manner possible considering the limited space available. Although it takes several days of preparation to clean them out, not one trace of straw, peanut shells, salt, or cow crap can be found when they drive up to the decorating area to be transformed into moving tableaux representing various religious and secular seasonal scenes.

The banks and churches sometimes have larger vehicles like the floats in the larger cities. It is Kellersville's best effort and folks love it. Marching units from surrounding communities join the local high-school band making it a festive occasion with renditions of the most popular songs and carols.

Although the high school sponsors a Christmas tree lot, many people still honor the age-old tradition of going into the neighboring woods to cut their own. Hank is one of these who wants a personal attachment to the cedar branch in the living room.

The next-to-last Saturday before Christmas he appears in the kitchen after breakfast with an axe and rope in hand to recruit PK and me for the expedition..

"Time for finding our tree."

"Where'll we go this year? To old man Sims'?" PK already knows the answer to this question.

"Of course. He always has the finest trees in the county."

"I'll get my cap and coat and meet y'all in the truck."

I glance up from my coffee mug where I've been trying to hide, "Y'all?"

"You don't want to disappoint your son in this family tradition."

"It's not a tradition in *my* family."

"It is now. Get up and move your lazy ass."

"Yes sir, massa Hank."

We cram in the cab of Hank's truck to the farm of Merton Sims, which, according to most people, always has a large selection of beautiful trees. Even though he supplies the local tree lots, he keeps some excellent specimens for the die-hards who want to chop their own.

After considerable looking and discussion about the merits of the crop, we narrow it down to two trees, both beautiful.

Hank is about to flip a coin when PK speaks up. "Why don't we take both trees, one for the living room and the other for Mom's room?"

Hank beams. He loves all the trimmings and tinsel that goes with Christmas. "That's a super idea. With the decorations already at the house and those I brought when I moved in, there's more than enough for two trees. We always have to leave some in the box anyway."

We chop down the trees and head toward the truck.

Hank and I are each dragging a tree and PK is walking behind us. Suddenly we hear a loud and unexpected grunt from the rear.

"Aw shit!" A half-screamed oath comes from the direction of PK.

We turn to see PK on the ground. He is obviously in pain. Since he is carrying the axe, my first horrible thought is he has cut himself or worse, chopped off his foot.

I throw the tree from my hand and rush back to where PK is sprawled and clutching his left ankle. As quick as I was in responding, Hank is the first to reach him. "What happened?"

"I stepped in a hole and twisted my ankle."

Hank kneels beside PK. "Here, let me take a look at that ankle."

"I think it's just a bad sprain, there's no indication of a break. I've got my first-aid kit in the truck. Don't move. I'll be right back."

Hank wraps PK's ankle with an Ace bandage and I help PK hobble to the truck. After loading the two cedars in the flat bed, we head back to the house.

When we arrive home, Hank immediately crushes some ice to apply to the injured area. As a coach, he is required to pass an extensive first-aid course—now he is again putting it to good use. Although it is evidently very painful, all agree there is no threat of fracture and a trip to the clinic is not in order.

"This brings up an obvious point. PK you are not able to go to Alex City to shop for gifts tomorrow. You'll just have to give Hank and me your list."

"Bummer."

The following day, Hank and I have conferences with both Nan and PK regarding what they want them to buy for their gifts to everyone.

I really want to get a sense of how much Hank and Nan are planning to spend so I can keep my gifts in the same price range. I don't want to stand out by over spending, especially since my financial status is a great deal more secure than theirs. On the way to the mall, I suggest a shopping plan. "Why don't we go together to buy the gifts for Nan and PK and then split up when we are buying each other's present?"

"And what makes you think I'm giving you anything?"

"Save yourself grief and make sure there's something for yours truly in Santa's bag. I'm a baby about Christmas."

"We'll see. After your trip to Atlanta, it may be ashes and switches. Were you a good boy?"

"I didn't hear any complaints."

"Speaking of complaints, I hope we don't have any problems with PK's list. He's so particular about picking out just exactly the right gift for everybody."

"I know. And he's very conscientious about spending his own money for gifts. I always send him a more than adequate monthly allowance because I know he saves money for birthday and Christmas presents. He gave me a list of what he has in mind for everyone and made me promise to spend only the money he gave me."

A day of shopping together is very revealing. I soon come to realize just how thoughtful and sensible Hank is. He obviously has saved some extra money and put a lot of thought into his selections. He and Nan don't have a lot of money to spend but spread it around to as many people as possible.

It takes all day to complete the list PK gave us as well as to buy for our own. Of course, the hardest selections are those for Nan. This will be her last Christmas and emotions are running deep. When we are buying for her, we both break into tears. The saleslady looks at us so strangely, we finally tell her the circumstances and she sobs the loudest of all.

The trip home is, thankfully, more upbeat. We talk about the gifts we purchased for everyone and how surprised they will be when the boxes are opened.

"I can't wait to see the expression on your face when you open my gift."

"Oh Hankie, I thought you weren't going to buy me anything but switches. I was already getting excited about how to use them."

"That still may be all you get. You'll have to wait until Christmas morning to find out."

"Christmas morning? We always open our gifts on Christmas Eve."

"I don't give mine out until the 25th. You'll just have to wait."

"Waiting isn't easy. I know, I've done it for years."

Although I mutter this last part under my breath, Hank obviously hears just enough to question.

"What'd you say?"

"Oh, nothing really.

We are right. Everybody seems genuinely delighted with their gifts. Christmas is very special! By New Year's, the trees are on the brush heap, the decorations are stored for next year, and Nan is worse!

Headin' Home to Hell

Part II

One

If It Looks Like a Duck...

Nan lives until the twenty-eighth of February. Thanks to medication, she has minimal pain. The following obituary appears the next morning in the Kellersville Tribune:

"Nanette Larsen Wolfe Warner, 36, passed away yesterday following an extended illness. She is survived by her husband Henry G. Warner, son Parker Larsen Wolfe, and ex-husband Harper Leroy Wolfe. She is also survived by her extended family members including Clairisse Wolfe Hopkins Mitchell, Charlene Hopkins Wilson Smith Howell, and Gerald Stone Hopkins.

A memorial service will take place on Saturday afternoon at 4 o'clock. Family visitation will precede the service at 3 o'clock at the Mitchell Mortuary on the Wedowee Road. The service will be led by Matthew Parks, Principal of Kellersville High School and the music will be offered by Ruth Ginsberg, Director of Music at Kellersville High School.

In lieu of flowers, donations are suggested for the Kellersville High School Library. Please send directly to the attention of Annette Farley, Librarian.

Interment following the service will be for the family only. Friends are invited to join the family at the home of Mrs. Clairisse Wolfe Hopkins Mitchell for light refreshments.

Services will be under the direction of Mitchell Mortuary."

When Hank reads the obituary aloud, I draw a deep breath of relief before I respond. "I wasn't expecting the memorial service quite so soon but it appears all of Nan's requested details are there. For once, Clairisse seems to be following someone else's wishes. And that worries me."

Hank agrees. "I understand your feelings about Clairisse. But in the long run it's probably better to get it over with."

"The only curious part is the mention of the interment. The only thing I can figure out is since everyone is accustomed to following the family to the cemetery, this will discourage one and all from parking their cars in the customary line up for the usual funeral procession to the burial plot. Anyway, everything else is according to Nan's instructions."

On Saturday when Hank, PK and I arrive at the funeral home, two of the assistant directors meet us as we walk through the door. They are the typical zombies who haunt the halls of this type of establishment to insure the activities go according to plan. The starkness of the snow-white heavily-starched plain-collared cotton shirts accentuates their black, single-breasted suits and creates the macabre appearance that is common to all in their profession; their lips barely separate when they smile to greet the on-coming men whom they instantly recognize.

One of them surprises me by speaking in an almost inaudible tone. "Good afternoon, gentlemen. Have we lost someone in our family?"

PK answers "No, we're all here. It's just the three of us."

Hank and I can hardly contain our laughter. Hank whispers to me behind his hand. "It's hard to tell them from their clients."

As they usher our trio into the family room, our guide instructs us, "Y'all can wait in here until the three o'clock visitation period starts. If there's anything we can get you, please let us know."

At this juncture, I think it's probably a good idea to reinstruct PK on how to get through these next two hours.

"Remember, just take it easy and realize that everyone will say wonderful things about your mother. They are not doing this to upset us; they just want to honor her memory. They've come to support our family at this time of sadness."

"I know, I know. But I don't want to do this. It's not what mom really wanted."

"Basically, that's true. But she did appreciate our Southern heritage and customs. She agreed to the memorial service and set the guidelines to her satisfaction. If she could deal with it, so can you. Don't forget. Say nothing about the cremation since it might upset some of the older people who don't understand."

"It all seems really stupid to me."

"Hold that thought to yourself please, at least until the services are over."

"What do I say to people?"

"A polite 'thank you' is a sufficient reply to most offerings of condolence. If at any time someone makes you uncomfortable by asking questions or saying too much, excuse yourself and go to the restroom to relax before returning to the visitation parlor."

There is a muted knock at the door and one of the directors comes to lead us to the family room. As we follow him down the hall, we notice quite a crowd gathered around the door waiting for us to arrive. Etiquette requires all visitors to wait for the family to enter first.

Clairisse, George, Charlene, Jerry and his wife, Suzanne, are all waiting at the head of the line. Naomi is standing alone at back of the others. We exchange nods, appropriately sedate smiles and clasp hands as we move toward the door. Clairisse, Charlene and Suzanne hug all three of us; George and Jerry give the usual masculine hand clap on the shoulders; the family enters the visitation room.

My knees almost buckle under my quivering torso. A cold chill runs up and down my spine leaving me as limp as a dish rag. I exchange glances of total disbelief with Hank. When I look toward my left, PK crosses his eyes and shrugs his shoulders in an attempt to communicate his total skepticism of the situation and to ask in the typical teenage body language, "What in the devil is going on here? Am I crazy?"

I quickly put my finger to my lips to insure silence. I turn to look again to reassure myself I'm not dreaming. The second glance verifies the first. Right smack in the front of the room stands a light-brown mahogany casket with a floral drape of yellow roses!

Then Hank and I begin a teeth-clenched, tight-lip, whispering exchange.

"Is that…?"

"No."

"I thought she was …!"

"She was!"

"Then who's…?"

"I have no idea!"

"What the …?"

"I don't know, but I know who's responsible."

"Clairisse?"

"Is there any doubt."

"None."

"Just look at her face. She has taken the throne and is receiving the faithful mourners."

"What's next?"

"Only Clairisse knows. Just be prepared for anything!"

People begin passing by the receiving line offering the usual condolences. PK seems to be in a daze. The casket is obviously too much for him to comprehend. I, on the other hand, have just figured it out.

I try to explain it to Hank. "Clairisse is probably just too embarrassed to let people know Nan has been cremated. She arranged this elaborate ruse to dispel any rumors of the unspeakable breech of Southern Baptist funeral etiquette."

I recognize a group of old women standing by the coffin: Margaret Simpson, the widow of the local cotton gin's owner; Harriett Jensen, widow of the controversial preacher who expelled the unworthy harlots from the church house; and her old-maid sister-in-law, Beatrice (pronounced *Bee-**at**-trice* like the small crossroads in south Alabama where she was born).

Since the initial rush of visitors has abated somewhat, I maneuver closer to them in order to hear what they are saying.

As I near the gaggle, Beatrice is reporting to the others, "I heard they had to have a closed casket because, bless her heart, she'd just wasted away to nothing and the make-up couldn't cover her washed-out complexion."

Harriett adds, "One of the pallbearers told Helen Johnson that when they moved the casket in here, it was so light they weren't sure anyone was in it. And Marianne Butler heard they had buried her in that pretty Alice-blue dress she wore to Charlene's last wedding."

Margaret calls the group of old ladies' attention to PK and Hank. "Poor boys. They look so worn out. Something like this just takes everything out of a body, especially the young ones who don't really understand how to cope with it all." When she realizes I'm not with the other two, she looks around and sees me approaching their group. "Harper, honey, we're just *so sor-ry*.

"Thank you, ma'am. We really appreciate you ladies coming to share this time with us. Nan would be so proud y'all are here."

I think about how long it has been since I have taken part in a Southern funeral and am surprised how quickly and easily I get back into the ritual. I'm actually reciting my part in the drama with ease. It is evident I'm still a Southerner, born and bred.

How is PK holding up?"

"As well as to be expected. Thank you for asking Mrs. Simpson. It is hard for him to realize all this is real."

"Give him time. He's just a boy. He'll be fine. They can all bounce back so easily, you know."

"Yes ma'am. Thank you for your advice."

Then Beatrice adds from the left, "The family spray is just lovely Harper. I know those were her favorites." (I remember how much Nan hated yellow. She always said it reminded her of jaundice.)

"Thank you, Mrs. Jensen."

I notice the women are edgy and want to move away from me so they can continue their "*funeralizing*" rite without the chance of being overheard by a member of the family.

As they move away, I overhear Beatrice as she leans over to one of the new arrivals. "One of the pallbearers told me that when they moved the coffin into the parlor…"

I edge my way over to the area where Clairisse is holding court. Trying to avoid attracting attention, I whisper through my teeth. "Clara, (she gives me the same disgusted stare every time I call her by her real given name) why is there a casket? I don't understand what's going on."

She responds through the black lace handkerchief she always carries to funerals.--Charlene calls it her 'funeralizing accessory'. "Honey, what's to understand? These folks are expecting a regular funeral."

"Who is in that coffin?"

"Don't be silly, honey! That box is as empty as a gourd."

"What if they open it?"

She dismisses his concern with an outwardly flippant wave of her hand. "Darling, why would anybody want to open it? Nobody really likes seeing dead bodies. The only reason anyone ever looks is not to be outdone by somebody else who *did* see the body. They don't want to be at a disadvantage and short end of the conversation at Belle's or Petersen's on Monday by not having an eyeball account of the deceased's condition. Of course, if the casket is closed, they'll all be in the same position; no one will know what the body looked like. All that will be left is speculation and the enjoyment of that lasts longer than the real information."

Hettie Lewis, the retired kindergarten teacher, a legend of Kellersville, enters the salon and waddles over to us.

Naomi whispers behind her hand. "Lord, that woman ain't changed a bit in all these years. She's just as low up and wide tall as ever."

Miss Hettie looks to be five-one in both directions. Her over-worked spandex pants emerge from the bottom of the caftan which miraculously rolls and tucks its way down the folds of her body to her pudgy little feet hanging over the tops of her Daisy Duck shoes.

Miss Hettie has long been retired but still talks to everyone as if they are her pre-school students.

"There you are my darling *little* Harper, we're all just so sorry about *little* Nan. She will be greatly missed."

"Thank you, Miss Hettie."

"How's *little* PK holding up? Does he understand what's really happening? Bless his heart, the poor *little* thing!"

"I'm not sure it has completely dawned on him yet."

"Harper, the family blanket is just lovely and the casket is very tasteful."

"Thank you, Miss Hettie."

"What is Hank (not *little* Hank since she never taught him) planning to do now that *little* Nan's gone and he still has the semester off? I wonder if…. Oh, there's *little* Marilyn Paulsen. Will you excuse me? I've been trying to get in touch with her for days. Yoo hoo! *Little* Marilyn. Yoo hoo, over here."

"Harper, Harper, Harper."

Even before I look up, that whiny affected Mississippi drawl transports my focus to that framed cross-stitch depiction of the *House of Seven Gables* which hung on Mr. Warren's classroom wall from those days of my junior year when I had such a crush on Fred Larsen, the first-string quarterback who sat next to me. Mr. Warren is now using a walking stick. I almost drop to the floor laughing; the cane is covered with a hand-crafted needlepoint case displaying his initials. What a queen. How did he ever make it all these years in Kellersville?

"Mr. Warren. How wonderful to see you again! Thank you so much for coming."

"I'm so sorry about Nan. She was always one of my favorites, you know. I brought her project to bury with her; *Hiawatha* was a wonderful piece of needlepoint and would have won that year if it hadn't been edged out by someone's *House of Seven Gables*."

"I haven't thought about that in ages." I tell this lie hoping my blush doesn't give away the fact that I actually remembered the horrible piece of rag mop at the PTA meeting several months ago.

" Have you ever done anything else?"

"No, Mr. Warren, I decided to stop with perfection. Thank you for bringing Nan's project, sir. I believe she would have thought this very special and would definitely want it to go right along with her." I try not to seem too condescending and would have probably made it with a straight face if Charlene hadn't giggled behind her **Keep Cool With Jesus** fan, the cardboard hand-held cutout on a wooden paddle which resembles an oversized popsicle stick and is the mandatory accessory of all Southern churches and funeral parlors. Her particular faithful cooling device is printed with a bust view of Jesus and His exposed heart, a common scene on the fans of the Catholic churches. As a matter of fact, these fans were acquired by the funeral home when the local Roman Catholic Church shut down the Mass it was trying to get started. The local diocese was so anxious to get a foothold in this area of the state, it jumped the gun by sending an itinerate priest to hold one service a month in the mobile-home meeting center the Seventh Day Adventist congregation used on Saturdays. It was not a good move since there were only four Catholics in Kellersville. They were "Yankees," of course. The father and mother of the family moved to town to work in one of the local restaurants out on the Wetumpka Highway.

Charlene nods in Mr. Warren's direction. "He had a garage sale two years ago. He had a stack of those shitty projects on a card table in the driveway. He had some nice things to sell, but the word got out that he wouldn't let you go until he rummaged through the pile and gave everybody their creation from years ago. By noon, the flow of customers dried up. Of course, when Harriet Thompson heard the news, she hightailed over to claim her prized whatever-it-was. That woman is a piece of work. I threw mine in the garbage and prayed the garbage men wouldn't refuse to tote the can away."

Mr. Warren changes his attention to the flower-draped coffin. "Oh my! What a coincidence! The primary color in Nan's piece is just the same yellow in those roses. I'll just put it on the foot of the spray. They'll go so perfectly together!"

Now I know why Nan had always hated yellow.

Clairisse puts the funeral hankie to her mouth. "See, I told you this is all an act. Everybody goes through the same worn-out old crap to play out the same tired old scene. It's like giving a party. If there's enough liquor and food, nobody gives a shit about the guest of honor."

I almost lose it and spoil the moment. In an effort to stifle hysterical laughter, I bury my face in my hands.

Beatrice, observing from across the room, whispers to the gaggle around her, "Poor Harper. It's just too much for him. He is so distraught. He still loves her, you know."

There is suddenly such a drastic silence followed by low but busy murmuring that I immediately fear someone has opened the casket and revealed the ghoulish deception that is being played on the mourners. When I turn to see the cause of the commotion, I come face to face with Pauline, Clairisse's granddaughter, and her half-black baby, much less acceptable to the citizens of Kellersville than a missing corpse.

Miss Hettie was the first to react. "Oh, there's *little* Pauline and her *little* …ugh…ugh…. Well anyway, there's *little* Pauline. How are you honey?"

In her flabbergasted state, Clairisse blurts out "What the hell is that damn girl doing here with that 'pickaninny'?"

"She and PK were very close when they were in school. I called her to let her know Nan had passed away," I blurt out almost gleefully.

At that moment, Clairisse rubs her arms and shakes her hands and feet. She seems to be feeling a tingling sensation in her feet and arms. Her head begins to spin and her body appears clammy. She looks around wildly as if she is searching for the nearest exit and wants to run out of the room. I know there are two gigantic reasons she would never run away; she is not sure her feet will support her body and more importantly for the simple fact that a Southern Belle never runs from a problem—she simply finds someone else to blame it on or deals with it.

Then it becomes clearer when I remember her similar reaction when I told her about Nan's desire to be cremated rather than buried in the traditional manner.

"Clara, are you all right?" I say with genuine concern.

"Yes, I will be fine in a minute. I'm just so shocked she actually showed up."

Clairisse screams through her teeth in the most contentious tone I can remember her using with me. "Why didn't you consult me before you asked her to come here? Why the hell do I have to spend my old age trying to out live the disgraces of my family?"

"I didn't think I had to request your permission because it is Nan's memorial service, not yours."

"Well, just look! Everyone's whispering behind their hands. They're making fun of us because the 'black sheep' of our family has returned—and I mean that *literally*."

"Mother. People will hear you."

"Charlene, I don't care if they hear me or not. I certainly don't want anybody to think I approve of this disgrace, even if she is my grandchild. I wish she'd take that little nigger bastard of hers and leave the state or even the country."

By this time, my temper, which I usually manage to control, is getting the better of me. I make no attempt to hide my anger as I snap at Clairisse. "That's their choice and not yours. She's here and you'll just have to make the best of it. So shut up and let's get this charade over with."

At that moment, PK has been over-exposed. He begins to shake, at first only slightly. Then as if he can no longer hold back the eruption of the volcano in his stomach, he begins to scream "You're all crazy. My momma's not in that box. She's not in that box. Dad, tell them. They don't understand. It's all a lie."

I immediately rush over to PK who is still ranting and put my arms around him and muster a calm tone. "PK, come with me. Let's go get some air." I stand up and gently move him toward the door.

Miss Hettie turns to the others and offers her take on the entire affair. "Poor *little* PK. He is so upset! He just can't face the fact that his momma is really dead. This is a typical adolescent denial tactic and it's a part of the grieving process. He'll be fine. It'll just take time."

Thankfully, Clairisse recovers from the physical manifestations of her anger and the visitation hour finally comes to an end. The funeral directors herd the group into the chapel where the sham continues to unfold. There, except for the coffin at front and center, the service goes according to the original plan. At the end of the service, everyone leaves—including Clairisse and company. The coffin has been the only real mark of defiance.

Looking back, I think I actually understand the reasons behind the deception. Having lived the majority of my life in this environment, I realize, regardless of the disturbing events of the day, a potentially uncomfortable situation has been avoided for the folks of Kellersville. In the long run, it will be for the best. Thank goodness since Nan never liked confrontations.

It also dawns on me that Clairisse must be full of herself at this moment because, in spite of all the directions and restrictions, she had been in total control— except for Pauline, of course, the one thorn in her side.

I actually smile at the thought of Clairisse's face when she first spied Pauline. I wish I had a picture of the occasion, but my memory will have to do.

Then I also remember Clairisse's violent reaction and physical discomfort. That genuinely concerns and surprises me. Hopefully, the last shocker of this trip.

Two

When It Rains, It Pours!—Morton's Salt

Hank's mind is still fuzzy. Since the "funeral" last Monday, he has been moving around in a fog of condolences and tears. Throughout all the complications and anguish of watching a loved one suffer and die, he has found strength and dependability in my apparent stability and seeming control of the situation. I genuinely believe he has grown to respect me and, who knows, maybe actually fond of me in a way that he doesn't understand. He knows from our conversations that PK is going to move to California with me. Even though expected, he feels another part of his world is being torn apart. PK is his last connection to Nan.

For me the tension of the last few weeks has taken its toll. During the entire ordeal, Naomi has been a godsend and taken many of the physical responsibilities off my shoulders. Keeping PK from freaking out has drained me of the last drop of energy. I came home from the funeral and collapsed. On the third day after the funeral, I feel I am on the verge of regaining my strength. Then the camel's back buckles under the weight of the last straw: Clairisse calls.

"Harper, honey, the day after tomorrow is Sunday and we're expecting you for the family dinner. Before you say anything, I will not take no for an answer. There's something very important we need to discuss so I think it would be best to leave PK at home this time."

This is it. She's moving in for the kill. It is time for her to reveal the next step in her scheme. My first impulse is to put her off, but I know from many years of watching her work an angle, the best strategy to find out exactly what she has on her devious mind, is to play along, at least until she reveals her plan. After all, there is no defense against the unknown enemy. Getting it out in the open will at least give me an idea of what I face.

"What time? Five thirty as usual?"

"Of course sugar. See you then."

The next move is to do what Clairisse herself would do if faced with this situation; pump the daughter for any glimmer of a clue as to her mom's design. This will require me to come up with my own devious plan to get her alone and press her for what she knows. I pick up the phone and dial.

"Charlene, this is Harper. I need a tremendous favor. I've got to go through Nan's belongings and decide what to do with them. I know you have people at the church who need things and I want her clothes to benefit the needy. Can you run over for a few minutes and help? I just can't face this without help. Hank, of course, is a basket case and would be worse than no help at all. Besides, I need an old friend at this moment."

I hope I have just presented her with an offer she can't refuse—an opportunity for first-hand information from inside the mourning family's house, a gossiper's utopia.

"Harper honey, you know you can count on me. I was just on the way to the Piggly. I'll drop by right now."

Hooked! All that's left is to reel in the catch. I have to empty the house of any witnesses; Hank has gone to the school. Nomi went home after lunch for the rest of the day. PK is at the library, the current social gathering spot for teenagers since there's no local mall.

Three

Digging

This is your cue Mr. Wolfe, I say to myself when I hear that familiar 'yoo-hoo' shrilling through the back-door screen like the guest of honor at a hog killing.

I take a breath as she walks through the door which I purposely leave cracked. "Charlene, I really appreciate your coming over. I knew I could depend on you. I don't know what to do with all her clothes. I know there are many needy women who can use these things, but I have no idea who can wear what."

"Honey, don't give it a second thought. I'll just take all the washables and let the girl do them and the cleaners will give the church a discount on the others. We'll probably send them down to Montgomery or over to Alex City. They'll just be so glad to get them. I don't think it would be good for PK to run into someone on the street wearing her clothes."

I respond without hesitation, "That part won't be an issue. Of course, PK is going home with me. We'll be leaving at the end of the semester."

"Not if Momma has her way about it!" The sheepish look on Charlene's face is as revealing as if a spotlight suddenly illuminates the depths of the darkest cave.

"And just what do you mean by that, Charlene?"

"Honestly, I'll just never learn to keep my damned big mouth shut. I don't know why I said that. Don't pay any mind to it."

"But you said it and now you have to finish. Explain."

"It just fell out. Momma will be furious if she finds out I said anything. Harper for my sake, don't tell her I blabbed. You know how she is. She'll kill me or at least make me wish I was dead, dead, dead."

I immediately went for the jugular. "Details, Charlene, details!"

"Oh Christ! I've already said too much. I think I'd better get out before it gets any worse."

"Charlene, it's already too late. You've already told it. Take a stand for once. Help me here! If you tell me what you know, I'll protect my source. Otherwise, I'll have no choice. I'll have to go directly to Clairisse. She'll definitely figure out it was you."

"Momma has been to a lawyer. She wants me and George to adopt PK."

I have to sit down before I fall down. I stagger backward and grope for the arm of the big easy chair which, except for the two occasions it was being reupholstered, has stood in the same location for the last forty years.

I finally regain my breath, but, unfortunately, not my composure and I scream so loudly and violently that it actually frightens Charlene.

"What the hell? Who the fuck does she think she is? What's she trying to pull here? Why does she think I'll go off and leave PK here?"

"Well, she thinks the judge will take custody of PK away because of your lifestyle, you know, your gayness. She doesn't think you should raise a boy being as you might try to turn him into one of your kind too."

"She is a stupid woman. I have known her to do some real shitty things in the past, but this is too despicable for even her. I was expecting something big, but not… (shaking my head in total disbelief) this."

"Just try to calm down before you stroke out and momma gets custody because you're dead and gone."

"She'll never get her slimy hands on my son." I jump up and fling my arms like a raving lunatic.

"Calm yourself. Don't forget. If you're **dead and gone**, she wins."

"Now don't you worry about PK. Of course, George and I will be so happy to take him. He's such a sweet child. We'll give him a good Christian home. George is so good with children. Anyway, she…."

I stand up and blurt out and interrupt, "Charlene thanks for your help with the clothes. Please take them and leave. I've got a lot of thinking to do. Don't worry. I'll not tell you said anything." I want to scream 'get out', but restrain myself. I am almost unaware of her leaving; my mind is running at high velocity—plotting.

I know time is short and there's much to be done. Planning and details are of paramount importance. I must have a counter measure worked out by dinner time on Sunday. I can not go there with **no** defense.

The first thing I have to do is to contact an attorney. I begin rummaging through the scattered cards on the dresser. What did I do with Paul's phone number in Atlanta?

Four

The Last Supper (Not a biblical reference!)

Friday morning to Sunday evening turns out to be at the same time the longest and the shortest period of my adult life. As I close the car door and walk up to the door, I remind myself to remain calm and collected. This will be a tactical game. It's important to stay in the cage until just the right time and not to end up as the canary in the cat's mouth. I inhale deeply, straighten my posture and ring the bell.

Charlene answers the door. The look on her face is akin to a deer's gaze in the headlights just before becoming the hood ornament. She manages a faint smile to accompany her greeting. "Come in. We're so glad you came. Momma, Harper's here. George, you remember Harper."

George, the quintessential Southern gentleman, stood and extended his hand. "Harper, we really appreciate the clothes. They'll come to good use for many needy people. I know Nan's spirit will rest better knowing they are going to a good cause."

"You're welcome. We're so glad they'll be used." My eyes sweep the room. There she is sitting on the throne; on her shoulders the customary black mantilla to ward off the night's chill. The rays of light from the floor lamp behind her head appropriately create an illusion of a giant spider web—the "Black Widow."

"Honey, we haven't seen y'all since the funeral. How're y'all holding up?"

"We're doing very well, Clara. Thank you for asking."

"It's just so sad. She was so young with her whole life in front of her. It just doesn't seem fair. Then who are we to question His will?"

How can anyone this evil refer to any God?

A grunt from the left calls my attention to Jerry and Suzanne on the sofa near the fire. Upon seeing me glance in his direction, Jerry raises his glass in an acknowledging toast. Remembering Jerry's taste for scotch, I wonder how many he downed in preparation for this evening. It is no secret he and Suzanne are ardent tippers under any circumstances. No doubt, they braced themselves well before their Sunday *obligation.* I certainly understand and considered a strong belt for the same purpose but opted against it in order to keep my wits at their keenest—I will definitely need to be on my toes tonight.

The evening progresses without any overt mention of the underlying theme. If Clairisse has any inkling I know about her plans, she gives no indication throughout dinner. However, since I am aware of her intentions, I recognize her carefully orchestrated prattle designed to set the stage for the main performance. I rather enjoy seeing how her mind works and schemes to finagle the conversation toward her agenda. For the first time I am really aware of her outstanding talent of manipulation; a real mule trader, she would have been very good at selling used cars. While the table is being cleared for the dessert, Clairisse makes a very obvious shift in her chair towards my direction, and I know she is about move in for the kill. I keep telling myself to get ready and stay calm.

During the entire evening she never mentions PK's name. Only Jerry and Suzanne ask about him. It is evident they have no clue about the plans. Both Charlene and George are visibly nervous when there is a chance PK's name would come up which means they have a script and are waiting to be cued.

Leaning forward with her left elbow on the chair's arm, Clairisse eases the conversation toward the subject of the evening. "How is PK doing in school this year?"

It's time. Patience is important. Clairisse must not suspect until she has revealed the full scope of her plan.

"Very well, as a matter of fact. I had thought he would be really bummed out over Nan and go into a trance. Actually he seems to put himself into his studies as a means of escape. In any event, he's doing better than any of us expected. Thanks for asking."

"Have you given any thought about PK's future?" she drawls.

"Of course; I've been planning and saving for his future since he was born. Just exactly what do you mean?" I decide to give her a little push.

"Of course I have no doubt you have made all the best financial arrangements, but I was talking about his personal well being. I don't think he needs to leave home right now. I've spoken to George and Charlene and they will be happy for him to live with them. That way he won't have to leave his friends and family. He'll be so much better off with them than Hank. After all, as they say, blood is thicker than water."

"Actually Clara, in your case blood is *deadlier* than water. I have no intention of leaving PK in Kellersville with anyone; especially under your control."

The smirk on Clairisse's face was too much to stomach. "Actually Harper, I've already talked to our family lawyer Clayton Small and he is sure Judge Peterson will rule against your raising PK because of your 'homosexualist' activities and that heathen California life style you lead. We have the papers already to send to the judge tomorrow if you try to buck me on this. I'm determined to see that PK will be raised in a proper Christian environment so he will turn out a decent man. If it comes down to you and the respectable preacher and his wife, I have no doubt you'll lose custody."

At this point, obviously feeling she has pushed the dagger in to the hilt, Clairisse sits back in her chair and picks up the spoon to taste the pie which had been placed in front of her, although it can't be as sweet as the taste of the victory in which she still languishes.

I lean back in my chair, take a breath, look directly at Clairisse and calmly start my reply. "Oh I can see you've been quite busy lately. You have, as usual, decided what **will be** without consulting anyone involved. You are so accustomed to running everybody's life according to your whims and getting away with it because no one dares to speak up against you. You suffer from the delusion that you know what's best for everybody else. You never stop to think anyone would challenge you and take a stand. You don't believe they can think for themselves. This time, your over confidence has left you quite vulnerable. All of your conniving and visits to the lawyer have been a waste of time. PK went to Atlanta this morning."

I notice a strange smirk of pleasure come across Clairisse's lips as I continue revealing my actions of the past few hours.

"I have no intentions of leaving him with this family. There is no way I can understand why you would even consider that Charlene, the playgirl of Randolph County and that grease-monkey-turned preacher husband of hers would be better fit to raise him in their so-called Christian home than I would. Not to mention your son and daughter-in-law, the town lushes who can't control their own child. They certainly are not suitable role models for any adolescent. Of course, none of them really ever had a chance to live their own lives with you as their mother."

I stand up, place my napkin on the table and look Clairisse in the eyes. "You've been out maneuvered this time. Learn to live with it!"

As I am walking toward the door, Clairisse again leans forward to deliver the final and killing blow. "Before you leave and drive all the way to Atlanta for nothing, you probably need to know that PK is in the custody of the Department of Family Affairs."

"What the hell are you saying?"

"Well sweetie we all know what a big mouth Charlene has. I figured she blabbed everything when I found out she went over to help clear our Nan's things. I asked myself what I would do in these circumstances and bingo! After that, the rest was easy. I got the judge to issue an order to prevent his being ushered out of the state. The sheriff caught Hank taking him to Atlanta. A non-custodial adult transporting a minor over the state line? Really Harper, I expected better attention to details from you."

"What have you done with PK? Where is he?"

"By now, he's at home with Hank. As you leave, Deputy Sims will meet you on the porch to deliver the court order to keep you from taking PK out of Kellersville."

"You're a class-A bitch, you know that?"

"Thank you, sweetie. That's the nicest thing you've said to me in years."

"If you liked that, you'd *really appreciate* some of the other things that have been said about you."

"Hush or you'll turn my head."

"This *will* go to court."

"I'm sure of it and look forward to it."

I turn and address the others. "None of you are safe. I'm going to fight for my son. Take warning, I won't hesitate to use any means necessary to beat this. I will destroy anyone and I mean **anyone** who gets in my way." When I say the last line, I stare directly at Charlene.

On the way out to the car, the deputy serves me with the court order. Round one—Clairisse!

Five

Everything has turned to S…!

As I wait impatiently for my call to be put through to Luke, a thousand things are whirling through my head. There was so much to do I don't know where to start. In this self-induced trance, I see myself as a fuzzy figure going through the events of the last few months of my life like a grade D soap opera on a cheap TV with bad reception.

Luke's voice interrupted my out-of-body experience. "I hope this call is coming from Palm Springs."

"Nowhere close."

"You sound agitated. What's wrong?"

"What's wrong? Someday I'll give you a detailed account, but for now, here's the thumbnail. Nan's funeral was a chapter right out of the Twilight Zone. People had no idea Nan had been cremated two days before and were hanging over the empty casket talking about her corpse just like she was there. My Aunt Clairisse arranged this charade to hide the cremation from the Kellersville's religious bigots."

"You've got to be making this all up." Luke responds.

"You haven't heard the best part yet. Last night I found out my aunt is trying to take legal custody of PK so her wild-life whore of a daughter and her ex-grease jockey Jesus-jumping preacher son-in-law can adopt him and bring him up in a *respectable Christian* environment that's free of, as she says, 'homosexualists'."

"Jesus, Mary and Joseph!" responds the voice over the phone.

"Thankfully I suspected something was in the wind and cornered Charlene who betrayed her mother like a Judas goat."

"So what are you going to do?"

"Well, there's more."

"I can't wait to hear what happened next."

"I planned a counter offensive in an attempt to outwit Clairisse. So yesterday, Hank was taking PK to Atlanta so I could get him out of Kellersville. I didn't think about getting the legal paperwork for a non-parent adult to take a minor across the state line so he and PK were detained as they were trying to cross the Georgia line. Of course, I wasn't aware of this, so last night, I walked through the gates of hell to confront Satan Herself with a water pistol."

"I have no idea what are you talking about."

"Thinking I had finally outsmarted Clairisse, I went to Sunday dinner at her house and had a showdown with my aunt that put the Gunfight at the OK Corral to shame—I lost!"

"What's the situation now?"

"Luke, when I was sitting at that table last night, I felt like a whore on the front pew of the First Baptist Church with last night's customer in the pulpit preaching against sex and evil drink."

After a pregnant pause, Luke says "Put that on paper and it will be your next best seller."

"For God's sake, Luke. The last thing on my mind now is writing. Clairisse thinks she's won. She has me dead and the hearse waiting at the curb. I've got to find a way to make the corpse sit up in the casket!"

"Have I missed something? Are you PK's biological father or not?"

"Of course I am. Don't be joking at a time like this."

"Harper, I'm not joking. The courts will never take a child away from his blood parent unless there's a good reason."

"Alice, wake up! You're talking about *Wonderland.* This is Alabama! I've come home to Hell!"

"What are you going to do? How can I help?"

"Get me a big advance on this book. I need all the quick cash I can get. Liquidating my assets is time-consuming and that's the one luxury I don't have."

"And just what do I use as the outline for the publisher? They're not giving an advance based on thin air. This isn't *Wonderland* either, darling. It's New York. And it's easier doing business in Hell than here."

"You said to write down my experiences here and I'd have a best seller. Write what I just told you."

"You're serious, aren't you?"

"You don't know the half of it!"

"I'll deposit fifty thousand in your account this morning. Consider it an investment. If you need more, just let me know. I'll get the proposal to the guys over at the publishing house by tomorrow. They'll eat it up. Don't forget any details. Take notes!"

"I won't need to write anything down. It's all too deeply burned into my mind. I'll have nightmares about it for the rest of my life."

"What are you going to do?"

"I've called and left a message for Paul Steiner, my lawyer friend in Atlanta. I hope he will soon be on his way here to represent me and PK."

"Speaking of PK, what does he think about this mess?"

"He's scared. And so am I. I don't know what I'll do if they take him away from me." I begin to choke my words and tears are flowing down my cheeks to my parched lips. "I just can't think about that possibility or I'll go stark raving mad."

"What else can I do?"

"Nothing right now. I'll stay in touch. And Luke, thank you for being a real friend. I'll love you forever for this."

I'm a little taken aback by the boyish feeling of relief when I answer the phone and hear Paul's voice on the other end of the line. I'm not sure whether it is from a professional or personal standpoint, but I immediately sense the childish warm flush of relief when during a nightmare, the light comes on and the comforting voice of a loving parent assures everything will be alright.

"Hi there. Sorry it's taken so long to get back to you but I've been back to Pennsylvania for a family wedding. I got your message about Nan. I'm very sorry. How are you and PK doing?"

"Until Sunday night, we were doing fairly well. Then, Snow White ate the apple."

What's up?"

After spending the next twenty minutes relating the recent events to Paul, I take a big exasperated sigh of relief. "I really need you."

"As a lawyer or a lover?"

"Both. I need you to help me keep my son and to be there with a strong shoulder."

"You've definitely got both of me. My last class is over at five on Friday afternoon. I'll leave from school."

"How the hell does one get to Kellersville?"

"Head for nowhere. When you get there, you're in Kellersville."

"Don't worry. We'll beat this together."

"I'm depending on it."

Six

Mommy Dearest

Hank's mother, Pearle, is a true belle of the South. Born and raised in Charleston, she attended the University of South Carolina in Greenville and graduated with a degree in French and Art. She met a career Air Force officer when he was the R.O.T.C. instructor at USC. Shortly after she graduated, they married. Subsequently, he applied for reassignment of duty and they traveled extensively throughout Europe until he was shipped out to Viet Nam. He never came back.

As a military widow, she and Hank were well provided for both financially and medically. Even though they couldn't live on base, they had commissary and PX privileges. Pearle was still a member of the women's groups at the Officers' Club and after a few years of widowhood, she met and married her current husband, an attorney in the Judge Advocate General's office. Hank didn't see very much of them because they both preferred overseas assignments and always requested them. They were being stationed stateside only because Jack was just a year from retirement.

When Hank arrives home, there is a message from Pearle on the answering machine. "Hankie, this is Pearlie. I'm really worried. I finally got your message about Nan's condition. We were en route to our new assignment. I've tried to call, but your phone isn't accepting incoming calls. It doesn't sound good. I've got a US cell phone. Call me, Sweetie. It's 707/433-6547. Au revoir."

In order to avoid unwanted calls for a few days, we had disconnected the house phone the morning following the infamous dinner at Clairisse's. Each of us had been using a cell phone for almost two weeks.

When we finally turn on the phone, there are a number of messages including Pearle's. Hank gets a beer from the fridge and settles down to give her a call. He recognizes the voice on the other end of the line and speaks in French "Bonjour Madame, je suis un pauvre étudiant qui travai…¨

She breaks in. "Where the hell have you been? I have had to call everybody from Mobile to Maine to contact you. The phone's been disconnected or something."

"Mom, we've been using our cell phones this week to avoid any calls. I've been trying to reach you. There's a lot to catch you up on. Nan passed away last week."

"Honey, I'm so sorry. I was afraid this was the reason the phone was temporarily disconnected. How are you and PK holding up?

"We're fine. I mean we were expecting it. I think PK is coping better than anyone anticipated. That's not the primary trouble at this point. There's too much shit coming down for a one-horse town. I'll explain when I see you. Will I see you soon?"

"This weekend. I've tried to make a reservation for a week some place near you, but I couldn't find a motel in Kellersville listed on the internet."

"That's because there's *not* one in Kellersville, listed or unlisted."

"Well, do something. I arrive at four o'clock Friday on Southern Air flight 20 in Alexander City, wherever *that* is. As soon as I get my luggage, I'll see you at the exit near the baggage claim area. Bye, bye, sugar." She hangs up before Hank can say anymore.

He turns to see me come in the room from the kitchen where I have been overhearing the conversation..

"Well, that was my mother. They have been transferred to a base in the US to finish Jack's time before the golden years. I've been trying to reach her to tell her about Nan, but because of their time in transit and our disconnecting the phone for a few days, we missed contact. She's coming Friday, for a *week*. I mean, I love my mother—but a *week*? Sweet Jesus, Mary and Joseph!"

"We'll make do."

"I'll see about getting her a room at Widow Smith's. I hope she has a vacancy."

I interrupt. "Don't be silly! She's family. She'll stay with us. She can have my room. I'll bunk with PK. We'll enjoy meeting and getting to know her. You've hardly ever spoken about her and I can't wait to meet her. Unless you think she would rather be at the boarding house."

"Please! She'll be in her element. She's a rare gem. I think that is why she was named Pearle. But, a week? Are you sure?"

"Say no more. It's settled."

Seven

Hurricane Pearle

To say that Pearle Masters is a surprise is like saying "Dubya" is a stupid man. Although I really had nothing as the basis of my expectations, I had formed a mental picture of a somewhat stodgy career officer's wife in her middle to late sixties who was accustomed to tea parties, receiving lines and military protocol. When she makes her grand entrance, I am open-jawed and speechless, which is quite an astonishment for a writer.

"Hello, I'm Pearle Masters, Hank's mother. You must be Harper. I've read all your books. You are so much cuter in person than in the picture on the dust jacket. I'll have a vodka, three cubes of ice and two olives, no pimento. Thank you for offering. Where's the bathroom? With these new baggage restrictions, they don't allow liquids in any container except the kidneys. I don't have a spare set and these have been working overtime."

I am still standing in the middle of the entrance hall mouth agape and wondering if she has taken even one breath during that spiel; Hank comes in with the bags.

"I see you've already met Mother."

"I'm not quite sure. Without stopping her pace or conversation, she introduced herself, ordered a martini on the rocks, three cubes that is, and beat a path to the bathroom."

"Don't forget the two olives with the pimentos removed."

"How did you know?"

"Some things never change, especially with Mother. I have the vodka in the refrigerator so it will be real cold and not melt the ice so fast; keeps dilution down to a minimum. I'm sure she would have mentioned it if she had not been in such a rush to get to the john."

Pearle whirls into the room. "God I'm so glad to get off that damn little plane. I bumped so much coming in on that little crop duster, I thought my bra wasn't going to hold up through it all. Of course, I've never had big enough tits to worry about them flopping under any circumstances." She gave a little laugh as she plopped down on the sofa. "Lovely décor, darling— it's so nice to see American furniture for a change. I swear it will be a long time before I sit on the floor again. Sober that is! Speaking of sober, where's that drink?"

"Right here, Madam. Pre-chilled, three cubes and two olives with the pimento pulled out. Make yourself at home."

"I already have, sweetie. Where's PK?"

I broke in. "He went on a field trip to the Shakespeare Theater in Montgomery. They'll be back around seven and Hank will pick him up while I cook dinner. I hope seven-thirty won't be too late for you to eat."

"Only if it's seven-thirty a.m. I will be perfectly fine as long as those *olives* hold out. What are we having for dinner?"

"Chicken."

"If you want it fried, it's my specialty."

"I don't want you to have to cook on your first night here."

"Honey, don't be ridiculous! I love to cook. Hank can still pick up PK and we'll cook up some chicken and get to know each other better."

"As long as the *olives* hold out?"

"Sugar, I love you already"

The three of us pass the next hour talking about the recent tour of duty in Japan. After Hank leaves to pick up PK at the school, Pearl and I adjourn to the kitchen to start the preparations for dinner.

Pearle takes the baton. "Sweetie, you do seem like something's bothering you. You want to tell Pearlie so she can make it better?"

"Is it that obvious?"

"Other than the glazed look in your eyes and the apparent distracted stare into space? No."

"It's a long story."

"Well, my olives are dry. Give them a bath. I've never been able to truly listen during a drought."

On the way to the bar to freshen her drink, I begin to highlight the events of the last few months. Only when I recount the story of the dinner with Clairisse does she begin to interrupt with questions for more details.

When Hank enters the kitchen, Pearle rolls two olives across the table toward him like a pair of dice. "Mama's had a pair. She's looking for three of a kind!"

"Where's PK?" I pipe in.

"The teacher called the principal and said they're running an hour or so late. Marlene Sanders said she would pick him up when she went to fetch Harry. In fact, she suggested he just spend the night over there since it would be so late." Harry and PK are best friends and are always sleeping over at the other's house. In fact, each household keeps spare toothbrushes and pajamas for just such occasions.

"Here's your drink Mom. If it tastes a little different, I used a new recipe I saw in Lucrezia Borgia's biography."

"Thank you sweetie, I've been simply **dying** to try it!

"Unless my arithmetic skills have decreased along with my libido and I've miscounted, there's an extra plate on the table."

I answer. "That's for Paul. He's going to represent me against Clairisse and those bastard cousins who are trying to take PK away from me because of my….."

"Lifestyle?" Pearle finishes the sentence rhetorically. My silence acknowledges her supposition. "It figures! Medical experts have made enormous strides in heart transplants—the *organ*, but not the *compassion*."

As Pearle and I cook, I catch her up on the family feud. I am just getting to the legalities when a knock on the front door announces Paul's arrival.

"Did you have any trouble finding it?" I ask expecting a not-at-all response.

"I followed your directions explicitly. Just when I thought I was hopelessly lost, I spotted the Kellersville city limits sign. Actually, it said 'Thank you for visiting Kellersville.' I had gone through town and didn't notice. In all fairness, it was the *edge* of town so there wasn't much to see."

I turn to face Pearle and Hank. "You've already met Hank. This is his mother Pearle."

"Hank, nice to see you again. I wasn't aware your parents were also from Kellersville."

"Mother just arrived this week. She's not from here."

"And, sweetie, you can take *that* to the bank!" Pearle waves the large cooking spoon in a circle and jabs it in a thrusting motion to make her point.

Paul laughs and speaks up. "What are the chances of a vodka , no vermouth, on the rocks with two olives for this weary traveler?"

"Oh I think we could manage to find that around here somewhere sweetie." She looks directly at me. "And while you're at it sugar, my olives are getting lonely all by themselves in this big ole empty glass."

"Taking her glass for a refill, Hank teases, "one more of these, ma cherie, and you'll be fried along with the chicken."

"Mommy will definitely take that into consideration sweetie. But from what I've heard tonight, a stiff dose of the potato juice would work miracles on some frayed nerves around here."

"Here, here," Paul chimes in with a raised glass."

"I didn't see a motel on my way through town or I would have gotten a room before I arrived."

"There's not one. Since PK's bunking over with Harry, You can share his room with me. It's that or a room at the Widow Smith's boarding house."

"Mmm, let me think about it!" Paul grins.

Pearl hastily offers, "I'd be *glad* to share my bed with you anytime!"

"All these choices make me feel so wanted."

Hank displays a grin that would make the Devil himself happy. "Or, I could share the room with Harper and you can have my bed."

I glance around and with a big smile on my reddish face, and grab Paul's luggage. "Butt out, both of you."

Eight

Facing the Facts

After breakfast, Paul suggests all five of us sit down for a planning session as soon as PK comes home. So, right after school, we convene around the kitchen table to plan our strategy.

Paul starts the meeting. "I think we ought to take a look at the laws in Alabama as well as previous cases in order to see where we stand."

"I agree. None of us have any idea what protection the State legal system offers or, for that matter, doesn't offer."

"Well, I'm afraid it's the latter case which is more accurate."

Hank speaks up. "I'm not at all surprised."

Paul continues. "Many states have adopted guidelines that do not discriminate against lesbian and gay parents based solely on their sexual orientation. (He picks up a law volume which has been marked with several note cards.) Alabama law states: 'The court may give the custody and education of the children of the marriage to either father or mother, as may seem right and proper, having regard to the moral character and prudence of the parents and the age and sex of the children; and pending the action, may make such orders in respect to the custody of the children as their safety and well-being may require.' Most of Alabama's neighboring states have followed this trend including Arkansas, Tennessee, Georgia, and

South Carolina. Alabama, unfortunately, has chosen the extreme opposite view."[1]

"Oh what a shock." Pearle rolls her eyes and tilts her head to express her astonishment.

Paul opens a folio and takes out a sheet of paper. "Just so you understand the full force of what we are up against here, I want to read you a synopsis of the most recent and probably the most publicized case in recent Alabama history. "

He begins "A lesbian mother who was living with her partner in Southern California petitioned the court to reverse the previous custody ruling in favor of the biological father. The Department of Family Services substantiated her claims that the three children had suffered mental and physical cruelty by their father. She contended that he referred to her in lewd terms in front of the children. In addition, he often struck them. As a result, they were having problems in both school and personal situations. The Alabama Court of Appeals found in favor of the mother. The father, however, took it to the Alabama Supreme Court and in 2002, the justices unanimously ruled in favor of the father. Chief Justice Roy Moore wrote a scathing diatribe against homosexuality in his decision. He described the lifestyles of gays as 'abhorrent' and 'an inherent evil,' which is 'so heinous that it defies one's ability to describe it.' He continues to assert that 'the consequences [are] inherently destructive to the natural order of society."[2] I could go on, but you get the idea."

"I think I read about this asshole in Japan. Didn't he get kicked off the Supreme Court because he refused to obey the Supreme Court of the United States and take the 'Ten Commandments' out of the courtroom?"

---

[1] *Lesbian and Gay Parents In Child Custody and Visitation Cases.* Kate Kendell

[2] *Lambda's Ethical Misconduct Complaint Against Chief Justice Roy Moore*. Lambda Legal Defense and Education Fund, 1997-2005.

"Yes, Pearle. The one and same. Also, he was soundly defeated in the recent gubernatorial primary. Even the radical right-wing Jesus-jumpers and bible-thumpers couldn't pull him through."

"I didn't realize there were still morally responsible people left in Alabama." I chime in.

"This is one of those good news/ bad news situations. The decision was nine to zero in favor of the father. Moore, however, wrote the decision based on his personal religious views. According to the other judges their decisions were based on the law and not religious beliefs. Still, the law is against us."

"So, what now?" I can't help but ask.

"Now," Paul answers, "we have to find a reason to give custody to us and not to them."

"Let's get at it!"

"Okay, I'm going to ask some questions that may seem dumb, trite and even, at times, too personal. I can deal with anything except surprises. When you go into negotiations or the courtroom and have them spring something new, the setback is sometimes critical and often times avoidable. You can bet the opposition is doing its homework and it will most likely come out anyway. Harper, we'll start with you."

"I assure you I have nothing to hide. Ask away!"

"Here goes. First are you the biological father of PK?"

"Yes."

"Did Nan know that you were gay when you separated?"

"Yes, definitely. It was actually the cause of the divorce." I spend the next few minutes filling Paul and the others in on the history of my life with Nan. Although I try to make it short, I spare none of the important points.

"PK, did you know your father was gay?"

"Well, I figured it out because of some articles I read about him, but I didn't know for sure until he told me a couple of months ago."

"Did your mother ever discuss this as a reason for the divorce?"

"No. She never really talked about it at all. Everything she ever said about him was good. She never said anything against him."

"What do you think about your father's being gay?"

"It's ok, I guess. I love him and want him to be happy. But I can't say I don't wish he wasn't. I mean, I wish he and Mom hadn't divorced and our family was, you know, the same as everybody else's. But I know it's not that way and we can't change it."

Pearle breaks in. "I'd like to ask an important question."

"Yes, Ma'am?"

"Do you want to go to live with your father?"

Throughout the entire six-month ordeal, no one had broached the subject of future plans, but we were all well aware of the questions that were running through PK's mind. This was the first time anyone mentioned the subject to him.

"To tell the truth, Ma'am, I've been thinking a lot lately about what's going to happen to me now that Mom has died? But do I really have a choice? I love Dad, but I don't know if I would like living in California. It just isn't fair. Moving to another school in a part of the country that is so different is really scary. I mean, I've got my friends here in Kellersville and I'm comfortable where I am."

In order to allay further tension, I speak up to address his primary concern as soon as possible. "Of course we'll be together and I'll use my last breath to make you comfortable. I can't imagine my life without you and I really hope you want be with me. If you don't, say it now."

"That's not the choice I want. No way I don't want to live with you, but why can't it be here in Kellersville?"

"I've moved on to another place in my life, PK. I don't want to come back here to live. It would be very uncomfortable for me and require a great change in my attitude toward living in the South again. But make no mistake about it, I *will move back here* if that is the only way we can be together."

"I just feel like my life is falling apart."

"A part of it is. We can't change that. I know it is difficult for you to have to change everything at once. But surely you can see this situation has changed Kellersville for both of us."

"I know. I'm just really bummed out about it all."

"So are we all, Son. So are we all."

Paul asks his next question. "Can you handle living with a gay man?"

"I don't know. But I *do* know I want to try. I certainly don't want to go live with *those* people."

"Thanks for being honest and open about your thoughts." Paul turns toward me and continues. "I've read the divorce degree and you're in the best possible position as concerns the terms. You are designated with *shared physical* and *shared legal custody*. Nan's having agreed to these stipulations in the divorce decree establishes her approval of your fatherly status in the years to come, regardless of your life style. It also implies her intention that you continue as *sole legal* and *sole physical custodian* in event of her disability or death."

"That's true. We discussed the future since I've been here. She naturally assumed PK would go with me. She also wanted me to give Hank a big kick out of Kellersville. She was afraid he'd chicken out and not carry out their plans to leave." He looked at Hank and grinned.

Hank broke in. "Nan and I also talked about what would happen after she died. She always assumed PK would go with Harper. She never expressed any concern about his lifestyle."

"That's very important. You will definitely have to testify to that end. Now that we have established Nan's intent on the custodial rights and responsibilities, we need to take a look at the law. Unfortunately, Alabama law isn't very congenial to gay parents and the precedents set by recent rulings aren't reassuring. This situation has one important distinction which may give us a faint glimmer of hope."

"And what is that? I'm beginning to consider a kidnapping and quickie jump over the border."

"We're not quite to that point—yet."

"Well, to what point are we?"

"Actually we are at a different starting point since the petitioner to alter custody is not a biological parent with legal custody. The way I see it is *they* have the responsibility to prove you are not fit to parent and that *they* are the only possible solution for PK's future."

Pearle speaks up in the matter-of-fact and blasé manner that each of us has quickly learned to expect from her. "We'll just have to find some dirt on them. Everybody's got something to hide. You just have to dig until you find it."

"Speaking of digging, Harper, this is the time to come clean if there is *any* incident in your past we need to discuss. Is there *anything* they can use against us to even *suggest* you are unfit to be a parent?"

As I am mulling over my years since leaving Kellersville, the phone rings. Hank answers. It is obvious by his facial expression the person on the other end of the line is telling something jaw-dropping.

"You've got to be kidding! That's just pure crap! Thanks for the heads-up."

As he turns to face our way, he is shaking his head and shrugging his shoulders. "Y'all are *not* going to believe this shit. That was Marlene Dawes, my colleague in the Math Department. She called to let us know they're holding a pray-in at the church tonight. They're going to have an all-nighter to pray for PK to stay with Charlene and George. There is already a group forming to march tomorrow on the square with signs in protest of the gay life style. And oh yes, it's a covered dish of course."

Paul has a stunned look on his face. "What the hell is a pray-in?"

"It's the cure-all for any crisis in a small Southern town, cook all day and pray all night."

"Well, while they are distracted preparing for this demonstration, we need to find out all we can about Charlene and George. Is there anything in their past that would cast doubt on their fitness as parents for a teenager?"

I hesitate for about half a minute. "There *is* something I already know but gave my solemn word never to reveal. If there is no other way, so be it. I'll use it if I have to."

Paul speaks authoritatively. "Well, you may need to plan on it. Don't wait until the last minute. We might be able to make a preemptive strike with whatever this is and nip this petition in the bud."

Hank breaks in. "What about her partner in crime, the Reverend George? How can you vilify a preacher?"

Pearle chimes in her two cents worth. "Honey, some of the preachers I've known have vilified themselves. And PK sweetie, (She waves her hand toward him and gives a grin that would have shamed the *Cheshire Cat.*) I don't care how long you sit here, I'm not going to give any details until you're older. So, what do we know about this… paragon of… *virtue*?"

Hank speaks up. "He came to Kellersville the year after I started teaching here. They said he was a traveling preacher on the revival circuit in Mississippi. Beyond that, I don't know much about his past. One thing for sure, he won't be opening up to us during this situation."

"Then we'll have to open this rat hole for ourselves. How do you get to this church?"

"What in the world is on your mind Mommy Dearest?

"Nobody here knows me or anything about me. I might find out some useful information by just mingling. Maybe I ought to *pray on it.*"

"Don't tell me you're going to church after all these years. Besides, they may not let you in."

"They don't know me from Adam's housecat."

"They may not know who you *are*, but they damn sure know who you're *not*. You're not one of them!"

"With all these dedicated gossips in Kellersville, no one will be able to resist the temptation to chat me up for the latest."

"Do you want me to 'wire' you for sound?"

"Now you're beginning to think like me sweetie."

Hank rolls his eyes toward the ceiling. "God help me!"

Nine

Looking For the Heel—
Achilles, That Is!

My mind begins to drift to that cold and rainy Friday in January of our junior year in high school. I had just stopped by my locker to get my literature book and meet Nan before the basketball pep rally. When she showed up, Charlene was in tow.

I took a deep breath. "Hurry up or we'll be late for the pep rally."

"We're not going. Don't ask any questions. Just get your books and let's go. Charlene, you go on to the car and wait for us there."

I knew this was serious because Nan never displayed the typical teenage flair for the dramatic that characterized the majority of our sixteen-year-old friends. She rarely kidded about anything. I closed my locker door, put on my jacket and followed Nan to the parking lot. From many years of experience, I knew not to ask questions. Nan would tell in her own time.

When we reached the back steps which led to the student parking lot, she motioned me over to a concrete bench under a leafless oak tree. After we sat, she quietly and calmly uttered the most horrible words anyone could have imagined in this time and place. "Charlene's pregnant and we need your help."

"Wow!" I was speechless for a brief moment. "Is she sure?"

"Yes. She's two months late and she never misses."

"That could be something else."

"She's got morning sickness."

"Oops! Looks like it's the real thing."

"Who's the father? Does she even know?"

"I didn't ask! It wasn't any of my business."

"Give me a break! She comes to you and tells you she is pregnant and you think asking an important question 'like who's the daddy' is too personal? There's a long list of possibilities from what I hear around school. He needs to take some of the heat."

"What a typical male response! Besides, that's not relevant at this point!"

"And why not?"

"She's not going to keep it!"

"Shouldn't the father have something to say about this?"

"I'm sure he would rather ignore the problem all together."

"How can you ignore a pregnant girl walking the halls of Kellersville High?"

"Harper, sometimes you can be such a dunce!"

"Ugh! You mean… *abortion*?"

"She got the name of a woman in Phenix City who does them for five hundred dollars."

"I hope you're not planning to borrow it from me! I haven't got *five hundred dollars*!"

"Relax. She took the money out of her savings account. All we need from you is to drive us down to Phenix City. Now, let's go!"

When we reached the car, Charlene was sitting in the back seat. She began to sob when I opened the door. I forced a compassionate smile. "Everything's gonna be okay Char. Does Clairesse know?"

"Oh *God* no! And **nobody** is going to tell her! Understand?"

"That's the first sane decision I've heard today!"

"Harper…, Harper!" Paul's voice jabs me back to the moment. "What were you thinking about? Want to share?

"I already told you there is something I know from the past and I promised faithfully I would never tell anyone. But times are desperate and I'll use it if I have to. PK, could you excuse us for a few minutes?"

PK, who had been standing at the end of the sofa, turned and sat down emphatically. "No way! It's *my* life and *my* future and I have the right to know what's going on. I'm not *budging*!"

"Well, I guess you're right. After everything else you've been through, you certainly ought to be in on the rest. I guess you all will eventually find out anyway, but right now I still can't say anything to any body but y'all. I made a promise and haven't broken it in all these years. I'll have to think this one out before I make it public. I can't break my promise unless there is no other way."

"This has got to be good. Wait until I make a little bracer for the unveiling."

"I'll get you one Aunt Pearle." PK gets up and goes to the bar.

"When Charlene was 16, she got pregnant and came to me for help. She had gotten the name of a woman in Phenix City who performed abortions and she begged Nan and me to take her to terminate her pregnancy. It was a medical disaster. As a result, she can't have children. The only thing wrong was she had to do it illegally and it obviously resulted in permanent physical damage. This wouldn't have happened if it had been done by qualified medical personnel and not a butcher. Nan and I have kept this secret all these years, but now the gloves are off. I'm sure this is all Clairisse's doings and I don't want to use this unless I have to. Besides, I definitely support a woman's right to make that decision. In any event, I'm not sure this would make any difference in today's generation."

Hank speaks in an annoyed tone. "Please! In case you have forgotten, this is Kellersville, *ALABAMA*. They're having a pray-in to organize a parade to protest your taking custody of your *own* biological son simply because they have determined you don't lead a decent life. Have I missed something?"

"No, Hank. Thanks for reminding me."

The phone interrupts us. PK, ever a credit to the American teenager, vaults over the back of the sofa and grabs the receiver in mid flight. "Hello."

"PK, is your daddy there?"

"Yes ma'am, he's right here." He puts his hand over the receiver and whispers, "It's Aunt Charlene!"

"Speak of the devil!" Hank waves his hand toward the phone.

I take the telephone from PK and speak calmly. "Char?"

"I hadn't got a minute, Honey, so listen quick. Of course nobody knows I'm calling. I just had to tell y'all it's not me! It's all Momma's idea."

"I figured that out already, Char."

"George, of course, is just like the rest of us. He ain't got the balls to cross her. I love PK and, of course, I'd be thrilled to death to take him if it got right down to it. I'd take real good care of him an' all. But he belongs with you. You've just gotta stand up to the ole bitch! I can't say anything to her. You know how she is! She'd make my life a livin' hell, not that she could do anymore than she already does."

"Thanks for calling. I really appreciate hearing from you. Char, I'll do what I have to do to keep PK and I think you know what I am referring to."

"I won't blame you. We'll always be…" She hesitates.

"Yes, we will."

"Bye!"

Ten

"Onward Christian Soldiers"

Paul, PK and I enter the back door laughing and joking.

"How did you like the Pig 'n Whistle?" Hank directs his comments to Paul who had earlier announced he had never eaten barbecued ribs. Immediately denounced as deprived and obviously in need of experiencing the ritual of the Southern male coming-of-age initiation, PK and I had whisked him away to local altar for barbecue worship on the Alex City highway.

"I can truthfully say I've *never* had anything so delicious! Of course, I'm a Jew and would hardly have *ever* found those delicacies on our dinner table. I'm sure the Star of David on my grandmother's tombstone spun like an out-of-control merry-go-round when I took that first fabulous bite."

I put my hand on Paul's shoulder to get his attention. "I didn't think you were religious."

"I'm not. My mother and father never practiced either. My grandparents, on the other hand, would have built their house on the Temple doorsteps if it had been possible."

At this moment, the front door opens. Pearle has returned from the "pray-in." She throws her purse and coat on the chair next to the cane chair next to the double French doors leading into the dinning room and heads straight toward the kitchen cabinet where we keep the liquor. "Honey, if I didn't already drink, I'd learn!"

Hank looks up from the Sports Section of this morning's *Montgomery Advertiser*. "That bad?"

"Not a word until I get a bracer. Don't get up, Sweetie! I know exactly where the *medicine cabinet* is. Care to join me?"

"I've already got a beer, thanks. But we may be out of olives. I used the last three in your go-cup for the pray-in."

"No chance! I have two extra bottles in my cosmetic bag, just for emergencies. How about you boys?"

"No thanks. We're still full from the beer and barbeque."

In a few moments, Pearle returns from her bedroom with the two largest bottles of olives available on the retail market.

"These should get me through the sideshow tomorrow."

Hank puts the paper down on his lap and looks at his mother through the corner of his eyes as if he is afraid to cast a direct glance for dread of the impending blockbuster announcement to follow. "Sideshow?"

Pearle takes a big swig of her libation, sits down on the sofa next to me and kicks off her shoes.

"Yes Honey, the carnival is coming to town. Tomorrow, they're planning to hold a prayer-sit-in on the town square. The church choir will start a sing-along at noon. The Reverend George will preach from the kiosk and a love-offering will be collected to offset any legal fees that may be incurred in the proceedings."

"You're making all this up!" Paul laughs knowing full well it's the gospel.

"The hell I am! I wrote it all down so I wouldn't forget any of the details." She pitches Paul an envelope that she had used for her notes. "Are you sure that beer's enough for you now, Baby Mine?"

After Pearle filled us in on the latest, PK clapped his forehead with the bag of leftover ribs. "Jesus H. Christ. I'll be the school joke with all this shit going on."

"Normally, PK, I would reprimand you for that kind of language, but when you're right, you're right!" I look toward Paul who appears to be staggering under the shock of such shenanigans. "Welcome to Alabama, Yankee Boy!"

Paul straightens up in his chair. "Pearle, did you learn any other information that could be useful?"

"Well as a matter of fact, I was introduced to the Reverend George, as Pearle Masters and he had absolutely no way to make connection between us. When I mentioned that Jack and I had been stationed at Greenville Air Force Base in Greenville, Mississippi, he really looked a little piqued. I'm sure he was more than a bit uncomfortable and hurried to change the subject."

"It sounds like we need to do a little digging for some of that 'Mississippi Mud' they used to sing about."

I speak up. "Actually, Paul, I know someone who might be a big help in that department. Harry Dennis, my college roommate and best friend for many years, lives and practices with his father-in-law in Itta Bena. I ran into his sister-in-law in Palm Springs not long ago. She works for *Palm Springs Life* and she interviewed me for an article in the magazine."

"My God!" Pearle clasps her hands together in a deafening crack that interrupts the conversation. "I haven't heard that name since dirt was new, Itta Bena I mean, not your friend. I don't know him from Adam's housecat. I was sure that little shit-hole of a town had vanished off the map!"

Hank turns toward Pearle in amazement. "How the hell do you know about that wide spot in the road?"

"One time, while we were stationed in Biloxi, I went to a couple of antique shops up there somewhere. Lord only knows how long ago *that* was! Actually, Kellersville seems like a metropolis compared to Itta Bena."

Paul turns toward me. "That sounds like a good place to start. Harper, if you'll give me the info, I'll call him tomorrow."

"Thanks, Paul. Just tell him things are really so complicated and I'm not ready to go into all the details with him right now. I'll call and fill him in later."

Hank speaks up. "There's something I've been thinking about since yesterday. I think you need to consider getting a local lawyer."

"Why on earth would we do that? Paul has a very personal interest in this."

"Yes, Harper, and that's precisely the point. He is your lover. I know this, Pearle knows this and most importantly of all, PK knows this."

"Oh my God, Harper, he's right. They will most surely question PK about your behavior. We can't ask him to lie and it would be a horror house blunder to have him point to me in the courtroom and identify me as your love interest."

"Jesus, I hadn't thought about that. Hank, I can't tell you how grateful I am to you for having pointed out this significant flaw. We'll have to be careful whom we pick. There is a good-ole-boy network here that would put the George Bush bunch to shame."

"And Honeys, that's saying a mouthful. Speaking of a mouthful, I've not eaten a bite except for a few skinny dry little ole olives."

PK points to the doggie bag from The Pig ' Whistle. "How about a few left over ribs?"

"I thought there was something smelling mighty good in that bag. Hand 'em over."

Eleven

"Blessed be the Meek" Does Not Refer to the Baptist

"Onward Christian soldiers, Marching as to war. With the cross of Jesus, Going on before:" The crowd is in full voice and responding in unison to the song director, a regular fixture at a Southern Baptist preaching, who is exaggerating his already arm-flaying style to attract the attention of even those congregants who arrived late and had to pitch their picnic tables and folding chairs around the periphery of the square. It's a spectacle for even the Baptists; signs and banners displaying slogans expressing the homophobic opinions of the people carrying them and, of course, various references to Bible verses which, according to usual fundamentalist custom, have been extracted, liberally paraphrased and applied to the appropriate occasion.

At first, I had absolutely no intention of presenting myself for public scrutiny. Hank generously offered to go and take pictures on the digital camera PK had bought to record our summer trips. But since Hank wouldn't know where to point the lens first, I decided to put on a cap and sunglasses and try to slip into the crowd.

I was initially shocked by the extent to which the church members had turned out for the occasion. Then I realized it was their chance for a "modern-day crucifixion" and they felt it their Christian duty to help drive in the nails.

At nine o'clock sharp, George steps up to the lectern which has been placed in the kiosk that usually serves as a bird roost. When it was installed last year, the original intention was to hold summer concerts. The only summer since the dedication was particularly rainy and the mosquitoes swarmed incessantly. Mosquitoes are the favorite snack for Purple Martins which, of course, arrived for the fortuitous banquet and blanketed the structure with droppings This, in turn, attracted flies and more mosquitoes. Under the circumstances, both musical performers and audience members were hard to come by.

George lifts his arms in the traditional palms-up come-unto-me gesture so common at the beginning of revival services. He speaks in the typical circuit tone. "Welcome to all and thank you for your commitment to this worthy cause. Let us pray! Oh God and Father of us all, we have come before You this day to beseech Your blessing on PK in his time of sorrow and need. He is facing a life which will expose him to the path of sin and depravity. He must be saved for a Christian life in Your service. He must *not* be allowed to be placed in the custody of his homosexual daddy. Father, we implore Your Devine Intervention in this matter. In the Name of Your Holy Son, Jesus Christ, Our Lord and Savior. Amen!"

The chants of *amen* roll through the crowd interspersed with a few *Praise the Lord*s and an occasional *Thank You Jesus!*

The song leader rises and lifts a card with large print to announce the next hymn: *Shall We Gather at The River.* How prophetic!

At nine-fifteen, the heavens open. The downpour lasts until almost midnight. Alabama needs the rain. The prayer session has been a success after all.

At ten o'clock, Deputy Perkins arrives at the house and serves a subpoena. I have been officially summoned to appear with PK for an official hearing next Wednesday. The gates are open; we're off and running.

"Harper, how nice to see you! How's PK holding up?" Theresa Lazenby, Amos Lazenby's secretary since God invented dirt, greets me as I walk into the office.

"He's doing real well, Miss Tessie Lou, thank you for asking."

A tall stately woman of advanced years, she takes pride in her appearance. Her perfectly white hair is rolled in a chignon to accentuate the look of professionalism projected by her navy suit and matching low-heel plain pumps. Born Theresa Louise Lazenby, Amos's elder spinster sister, she attended the University but dropped out after marrying a fellow student in her first year at the Law School. After an unhappy divorce, she took back her maiden name, returned to Kellersville and began work as Amos's assistant.

"I know Nan's passing has been hard on all of you. And now this thing with Clairisse."

"Yes ma'am. It is a terrific pain in the you-know-what."

"Well, she's always been one of those."

"Amen." Amos pops out of his office. "Harper, come on in."

Miss Tessie Lou follows them with her steno pad and takes a seat in the chair to the right of Amos's desk. "Harper, can I get you anything?"

"No thank you."

Amos opens the conversation. "After you called yesterday, I pulled a copy of the Divorce Decree I prepared for y'all five, well now almost six, years ago. I see in my notes that Nan was very specific about your remaining an integral part of PK's life and upbringing. In fact, as is my usual custom, I had her sign the transcript of our meeting regarding the details of the petition. I do this to insure I have done everything according to the petitioner's instructions. This way, I can testify that she was not antagonistic to your lifestyle. This was clearly spelled out in our discussion but she adamantly refused for it to be mentioned in the petition for separation. She also designated you with Joint Physical Custody and Joint Legal Custody."

"That was also my understanding."

"I've looked over the summons you slipped under the door yesterday. They've really done their homework on this one."

"Yes, I know it's very thorough. My friend Paul Steiner, an attorney and Law professor at Emory, was visiting over the weekend. He read it and commented we certainly had a challenge ahead of us. By the way, we're personally involved."

"I figured that."

His candor is surprising. "How so?" I ask to register my surprise.

"No one in his right mind comes from Atlanta to Kellersville for the weekend unless there is a very special reason. And of course, this is *Kellersville.*"

"I should've realized."

"Let's look at the official petition and then we'll take each point individually. As you must know by this point, the courts have the power to modify the original child custody arrangements if there has been a substantial change in the status of the parents and/or the change results in something negative the child's environment and that the juvenile is endangered by this circumstance. The party petitioning for a custody modification must prove the accusation and also that he or she can provide a better environment for the child."

Miss Tessie Lou has two copies of the summons. She hands me one and keeps the other. Amos starts to read from the original petition.

"Point One states that a substantial change has occurred as a result of Nan's death. This, of course, is an irrefutable claim."

"Without a doubt," says Miss Tessie Lou.

"Point Two is also undeniable and therefore we don't need to spend much time on this. There will be a required geographical change which entails schools, friends and different living environment. California schools are generally considered more advanced than Alabama schools, so this would be an improvement for PK. The social void created by the loss of his life-long friends will be difficult to overcome unless PK is excited about a re-location and starting over."

"I really don't know the answer to this one," I answer hesitatingly since I'm not sure if Amos is looking for my input at this point or simply asking a rhetorical question. "He hasn't said much under the circumstances."

Miss Tessie Lou confirms her agreement with the proverbial Southern expression in these situations. "Bless his little heart."

Amos moves his gaze from me to his sister and back again to the paper. I take this gesture as his tacit implication that he is not amused by the frequent interjections of our opinions and comments. "Point Three is more complicated. Here they assert that your alternative lifestyle of sexual promiscuity endangers PK's emotional well-being because it subjects him to peer embarrassment by living with a gay man, especially his father; in other words, emotional abuse. An important factor is the juvenile's awareness of the sexual misconduct.

"Now, Harper, you must maintain your composure at this next accusation. Point Four raises the possibility of physical abuse by you and or your friends."

"Those are the stupidest people in the world if they think I would ever…"

"This will be the hardest to counter since general fundamentalist principles have established these fears deep in their rhetoric. So let's start with the hardest. Does PK know you are gay?"

I hesitate momentarily to see if he is expecting an answer. I take a chance and reply. "Yes, I had a long talk with him several months ago. It was really no revelation since he had already figured it out."

"What was his reaction?"

"Well, I'm not going to delude myself into thinking he is happy with the fact that his father is gay. I do, however, feel strongly he is prepared to adjust."

"The courts are not bound by the wishes of the juvenile, but since PK is over the age of twelve, his desires should definitely be considered and weighed heavily. We need to get him to sign an affidavit stating his preference for living with you."

"I'll discuss this with him when I get home."

"Actually, I think it would better for me to talk to him personally so I can truly say I know what he wants."

"I understand."

"Point Five avers that emotional damage will result from his exposure to your, and I quote 'unhealthy, promiscuous and morally reprehensible lifestyle which you follow in your pursuit of homosexual contacts to gratify your abnormal sexual urges.'"

"Oh that's a nasty one," gasps Miss Tessie Lou as she fans with her steno pad.

"You're right Miss Tessie Lou. It's a low blow under any circumstances." I turn and direct my next comment to Amos. "How much of this does PK have to hear in detail?"

"That depends on the director of the inquiry or judge if it gets to the courtroom. I will petition for PK to be excused for everything except his direct questioning, but since he has just turned fifteen and we are submitting his affidavit for custodial preference, I'm not sure how successful it will be."

"Is PK aware of any of your affairs or friends?"

"Yes. Although he has never seen me in any intimate contact with anyone except his mother, he is very aware of my special relationship with Paul Steiner."

"Your lawyer friend from Emory?"

"Yes."

"And what is his reaction to Paul?"

"I think he's starting to warm up to him."

"By that you mean he's not thrilled with it?"

"Right. I've concluded that PK is insecure at this point and his less than ecstatic reaction to Paul is a result of this uncertainness."

"I'm not passing judgment, but it is a factor we need to consider."

"I understand. Paul wants to take an active role in the legal matters but realizes how unethical it would appear under the circumstances."

"Well, that's very level headed on his part. I can only imagine the field day their lawyer would have with your lover as defense counsel."

"How does it look to you so far?"

"Touchy."

"What next?"

"Send PK in around two this afternoon."

"Agreed."

As I am leaving the office, Miss Tessie Lou puts her arms around me and smiles as she offers a comforting word. "I just know Amos will get this all worked out. Don't worry."

Eleven

Madame… EX?

When I enter the room with PK, I am astounded by the number of people already seated in the small space allocated for observers. There is no sure-fire way to know how many had come to participate in the hearing or just for the curiosity. After all, the official pastime of Kellersville is "information processing" and this is *definitely* the best show in town.

As we proceed toward our seats in the front, Mrs. Dobbins stands and waves a little envelope to attract my attention. I smile and walk over to take the note from the self-proclaimed first lady of Randolph County because I suddenly realize each and every member of *Les Dames* is seated in the second row.

"Keep heart, Harper. You have more friends than you think."

"Thank you, Mrs. Dobbins. Thank you all!"

"I'm sorry you have to go through all this. The Baptists are always causing problems over their fundamental beliefs. We are all Episcopalians and more civilized, you know. Except for Agnes, that is, and she's a Presbyterian, but then, nobody is perfect."

When I sit down, I open the envelope which had been embossed with "Les Dames" on the black flap. A hint of a tear began to form in the corner of my eye as all the *Dames* nod and smile.

"Harper, you have our admiration, respect and support. Sincerely, Eleanor Dobbins." Southern women of social standing always sign notes, formal and informal, with their first and last names lest they be thought too condescending and snobbish.

Paul is just entering the room when the judge opens the chamber door and enters. She's not from Kellersville. The closest Family Court is located in Wedowee, the County Seat and therefore Ms. Emily Rosenberg, an appointed officer and representative, has come to determine if the petition merits a full hearing at the county level. Often this pre-trial inquiry arbitrates many disputes thereby saving time and money for the court as well as all the parties involved.

Ms. Rosenberg, a small-framed woman with well groomed grey hair, is not wearing a robe. Her tailored navy pantsuit is very simply accessorized. Before she sits, she speaks. "I must remind you this is not a trial. It is merely an informal investigation to establish a need, or lack thereof, for a formal inquest at the county level. We will, however, follow a procedure to arrive at a solution at the local level or remand to further judicial action. Please be seated. We'll hear from the petitioners first."

Herman Stokes, one of the most prestigious lawyers in town, rises to his full five foot three inches and faces Ms. Rosenberg. He is really only five-two, but when he lifts himself on the balls of his platform shoes, he not only looks a little taller, but also feels more important.

He opens his mouth to speak in his exaggerated drawl for courtroom effect. "Yo Honna, we are here on the behalf of the Reverend and Ms. George Howell. We feel the minor child, Parker Lee Wolfe, will have a more healthy and fit upbringing in a good and stable Christian home rather than being exposed to the unsavory and sinful lifestyle of his homosexual biological father. The boy is at a very impressionable age and being parented by a practicing sexual deviant will not only subject him to possible physical molestation, but also emotional embarrassment in his peer relationships. We are interested in only the best for the adolescent and definitely feel this is available in the Christian family environment of the Howell home. Ms. Howell is a well-known and respected life-time resident of Kellersville and of, of course, her husband is the pastor of the largest church in the community. They will provide the opportunity for the young man to continue living with his family and friends in Kellersville where he has spent his entire life. Thank you."

Amos Lazenby stands quietly and smiles politely. He takes two small steps toward the front desk. "I represent Parker Lee Wolfe and his father, Harper Styles Wolfe. Mr. Harper Wolfe is the biological father of PK, the *boy* in question. When Harper and Nan, his now-deceased spouse, separated five years ago, the divorce decree granted in Randolph County in the State of Alabama, invested Harper Wolfe with *Shared Physical* and *Shared Legal Custody*." He looked at Ms. Rosenberg and continued. "I'm sure you have already reviewed the legal decree." She nods in agreement. "I certainly hope you found it in good legal order since I was the attorney of record. Therefore, I can attest to the intent of all parties involved. This was just over five years ago, right after my learned opposing counsel moved to Kellersville from another state, somewhere to the west." In Kellersville, it never hurts to emphasize someone's non-native status when trying to better them in a war of words.

Amos shifts his stance only slightly and continues. "Ma'am, I wonder if now is not a good time to hear from the young man whose future is being decided here today."

He has decided to preempt the petitioner's calling PK so that he can be the first to ask the questions. Ms. Rosenberg nods her approval.

"PK, please come up and take a seat in this chair at the end of the table."

Amos starts the questioning with a direct approach. "PK, did you know your father was gay?"

"Yes sir." Amos had told PK to answer the question truthfully but not to say anything other than the answer.

"How long have you known this?"

"Last year, I read an article about him on the internet. But he told me one night right before Christmas."

"How do you feel about the fact that your father has special friendships with other men."

"I don't really know that I've thought about it that way. I mean, I *know* what it means, but I've never, you know, like…really *thought* about it."

"I understand. Since he and your mother divorced, have you seen him a lot?"

"Well, we always spend a week at Easter and a month together in the summer. We go for special trips. I plan them and we have a great time. We email every week and he sends my allowance every month."

"When you and he are together, does he ever leave you alone at night to go out to a party or to a nightclub?"

"No sir, never."

"Did you notice anything unusual that would cause you to think he was gay?"

"No sir."

"On your trip to the horse ranch last year, did your father make any special friends?

"Well, I didn't know it at the time, but he must have."

"Why do you say that?"

"That's where we met Paul and his daughters."

"And who is Paul? Is he here today?"

"Yes sir. He's right over there."

"Do you know if your father has seen Paul since the horse ranch?"

"Yes sir. Twice that I know of."

"And when was that?"

"The first time was last December. He went to Atlanta for the weekend."

"How did you know he visited Paul?"

"I didn't know for sure. He never said what he did there. I just assumed they visited."

"Why did you assume that?"

"Well, the next week when we went on the RV trip to Asheville, Paul called and met us in Cashiers."

"Was there anybody on the trip besides you and your dad?"

"Yes sir, Hank went with us."

"Were you happy Paul came?"

"Not at all. It was our time, we didn't invite him. I didn't want him to come."

"Did he stay in the RV with the three of you?"

"No sir. He stayed in the hotel."

"Did your father spend any time alone with Paul? Did he spend the night with him?"

"No sir."

"Do you like Paul?"

"I didn't at first, but after that trip, I sort of got to like him more."

"What do you think is the relationship between your father and Paul?"

"I think they're trying to be good friends."

"Would you feel funny about living with a gay man?"

"I don't know. But I *do know* he's my father and I love him. I want to live with him, not here with Charlene and her husband. They're so weird. And Aunt Clairisse… well, everybody knows she's mean."

"Thanks, PK."

"It seems to me there is no question here. Mr. Wolfe is the biological father and legally he has both *Shared Physical* and *Shared Legal Custody* according to the terms of the officially adjudicated divorce degree. So far, the petitioners have nothing to substantiate their claim to modify custody except their inferred unacceptability of my client's *supposed* life style. They claim…"

Herman Stokes stands up, rises up on his toes as usual and asserts with a sinister grin, "Pardon me for interrupting, Your Honor, but I would like to remind you that he *is a known homosexual;* and you know what *that* means!"

"First of all Mr. Stokes, do not address me as 'Your Honor'. I am not a judge and this is not a formal hearing. Secondly, I'm well aware of what the word *homosexual* means."

"Of course, Your…Ms. Rosenberg."

"Mr. Lazenby, please continue."

"Thank you ma'am. As I was beginning to point out, they have not proved Mr. Wolfe would be an unfit parent. But I really think we should look at the home environment they are proposing as the 'appropriate' home life for PK. Could we please hear from Mrs. George Howell?"

Charlene stands up and starts to move toward the chair next to Ms. Rosenberg.

"Ma'am, excuse me. I was referring to the LEGAL Ms. George Howell."

Charlene stops dead in mid stride. There is an instantaneous burst of gasps exploding in the room followed almost immediately by a grave-yard-at-midnight void of silence. People can't decide where to look—first to Charlene, then to George, back to Charlene, to Clairisse, back to George…and finally fix on the woman making her way to the front of the room.

The very ordinary appearing woman is dressed in a plain cotton dress, flat shoes and carries a manila envelope. At this point, she is anything but ordinary—she is obviously claiming to be Ms. George Howell.

Clairisse blurts out, "Who the hell is she?"

Charlene grabs for the nearest chair. George's face is ashen.

Emily Rosenberg pulls her small-framed glasses down on her nose and utters the only words that came to her mind, "My, my, my, my, my! This is definitely worth the trip from Wedowee!"

Herman Stokes half rises in his seat. "Can we have a short lunch break?"

Emily Rosenberg shakes her head. "Not now, it's just getting interesting! We need to find out the identity of our mystery lady. Don't keep us in suspense! Who are you?"

"I am Margaret Bates Howell. George Howell is my husband."

George jumps to his feet. "The hell I am. We're divorced."

"Actually, I never signed the papers and didn't file them. We're still married!" She hands the file to Emily Rosenberg.

Clarisse screams, "I don't know who hired this bitch, but she's a damned liar. They've just got her here to make us look bad!" Clairisse is almost frothing at the mouth. She can't sit still. Herman Stokes puts his hand on her arm in an effort to calm her down, but it is useless.

Finally Ms. Rosenberg finishes reading the contents of the file, places it on the desk, removes her glasses and leans forward to prop her chin in the palm of her hand which is supported on the desk by her elbow. "I have an official copy of the marriage license and the page of the county record in Mississippi where it was recorded. I also have the original petition for divorce of George and Margaret Howell. It has been signed and dated by George, but the signature line next to Margaret's name is *blank*! There is no indication the divorce was ever legally filed. Reverend Howell, it appears you are a bigamist! I'm sure the District Attorney will be in touch! Since the Christian environment proposed for the minor is in question and I see no indication that Mr. Wolfe is incompetent to raise his son, I am advising the petition be denied."

Charlene turns to George and plants her fist square on his jaw with such force that he falls over backwards in his chair. She moves toward him, steps over the chair, puts her foot in the middle of his chest and screams, "Get up you sanctimonious shit and let me flatten your slimy ass again. Didn't you ever bother to find out whether she even signed the goddamn papers or not? All this time, we've not been married, just living in sin and bigamy!"

"Aw, get over it Charlene. You screwed just about every man in town before you met me and never worried about marriage then."

"And they were *all* better sex than you! I never wanted to marry you anyway. It was all Mother's doings. You weren't such a good catch, just the only middle-aged eligible bachelor in town. Oh, *excuse me*! Did I say *eligible*?"

"You think you were such a bargain? Your dear mother paid me twenty thousand dollars to marry you. You don't *actually* think I'd have fallen for all that 'save my soul shit' you spouted if I hadn't been in on the act! What do you think I am, stupid?"

"You're the one who thought you were divorced, not me! I never even knew you'd been married before. I can't believe there's anybody else that would have you. In fact, I can't think of any reason I let Mother talk me into it for *any* reason!"

The other people in the room are paralyzed and stupefied. On the one hand, they want to dash to the nearest phone to be among the first to spread the news. On the other hand, they can't pry themselves from this unfolding family massacre, which is definitely better than the goriest highway accident.

Clairisse jumps to her feet and screams at George. "You son-of-a-bitch. You're not fit to preach much less be a parent. I'll take the boy. I'm not giving him up to that queer! Neither of you has any Christian decency! I've spent all my adult life trying to out live the embarrassment this family has caused. I have a sot for a son and daughter-in-law, a queer nephew, a half nigger for a grandbaby, and now, I find out my whoring daughter is a bigamist. At least we don't have a Jew in the family." Her face glows the color of a fire engine and running with sweat. She is almost racing in small circles and flaying her arms as she continues to scream. Suddenly, she grabs her temples with both hands and falls to the floor.

Poor PK's face can't hide his panic from the hysteria of the moment. Never in his fifteen years had he ever seen this kind of behavior, not even on TV or in the movies.

I keep my arm around PK in an effort to calm him through this frantic scene. "Paul, you are full of surprises! How did you ever…?"

"You can thank your friend, Harry Dennis. He dug all this up and brought George's wife over here this morning. He and Helen are waiting in the back of the room to see you. They didn't want to come up too early and spoil the surprise effect."

Glancing toward the rear of the courtroom, I see my best friend from college and his wife, Helen who looks as if she is ready to deliver an elephant. My friends smile, wave, and move toward the three of us. As they approach, Harry speaks first. "Well ain't this a change; *my* coming to *your* rescue for once. I've been owing you one for years!"

"You came through big time. How are you two? I see you're adding another one to the family."

"Well, actually it's two this time."

Helen hugs and turns to face PK who is still having a hard time putting everything into perspective. "Honey, we're so sorry about your momma. We had no idea she was sick."

"Thank you ma'am."

"Why don't we get out of here and go get a 'cocola.' The men can tie up all the loose ends and catch up with us in a few minutes."

"Thank you ma'am!" PK and Helen turn to leave.

The paramedics arrive within what seems to be only seconds; the firehouse is next door. They manage to stabilize Clairisse and transport her to the local emergency clinic where the doctor determines she has suffered a massive stroke.

Epilogue

One

Like Mother, Like Daughter

The Reverend George resigned from the church and left town before the tar could be heated and the feathers plucked. The first thing next morning, after leaving his resignation letter on the desk of the church office, he went to the bank to withdraw money from their account; he was an hour late and definitely more than a dollar short. Charlene, a personal friend of Ned Hargrove, the bank president, arrived before business hours and closed the household checking and savings accounts and emptied the safe-deposit box. He was stunned to find out the *secret account* where he had hidden the "dowry" money had been closed last year by Clairisse—not necessarily an approved banking practice, but Kellersville is a small Southern town and Clairisse, although not personally popular, was financially powerful because of the family business.

When George walked out the bank's front door, he was greeted by the sight of his car hoisted on the back end of a tow truck. On the sidewalk, a small crowd had gathered to find out what was going on in this bizarre scene. George was speechless. He was fuming! He had no alternative but to start walking.

The first thing he noticed on the front porch was a suitcase. His clothes had been packed and left on the porch. An envelope had been scotch taped to the top of the luggage: inside, a Greyhound ticket to Montgomery, a hundred dollar bill and a note. "This is more than you deserve, but I didn't want you hanging around until the sheriff caught up with you. He'd put you in jail and you'd be here for too long. This way, you can get your sorry ass out of my life!"

At first, Charlene didn't attend social functions for several months, not so much because of the embarrassment of being in a bigamist relationship with the preacher of the largest congregations in the county, but because the combination of Clairisse's stroke and the day-to-day operation of the family business consumed all of her time.

As a result of the stroke, Clairisse was partially paralyzed. Although she had lost complete function of the right side and her left leg, her mental faculties were miraculously unimpaired and, much to everyone's great disappointment, her speech function remained in good working order. She still delivered her demands and opinions with as caustic a tongue as ever.

Charlene, much to Clairisse's objections, put her mother in a nursing home. She informed the staff that she was paying the bills and therefore would make **all** the decisions regarding her mother—no one told Clairisse.

The screaming cat fights at the nursing home between Clairisse and Charlene became legend in Kellersville and a regular topic at Belle's on Monday mornings. The patient was pleased by absolutely nothing her daughter did, and she didn't hesitate to make everyone aware of her displeasure. Charlene, on the other hand, appeared to relish each opportunity to let her mother know she was in control. She could and would do to please herself and Clairisse had absolutely no recourse.

Although Charlene very felt secure in her position, she was still nervous about her trip to the home this morning to get Clairisse to sign over legal control of the business and family affairs.

As she entered the front door of the wing where Clairisse's room was located, she was greeted by the attendant who had just cleaned her room. "Good morning Hazel. How's our patient today?" Hazel Green and Charlene had gone to school together all their lives. Hazel was the sweet chubby girl whom everyone liked because of her fantastic personality. She had been assigned to Clairisse because of her size. Clairisse, as a result of her paralysis, had to be physically handled for all of her daily functions.

"Morning, Charlene. I just cleaned up the room and brought her breakfast. I don't reckon she's eaten a speck yet. She won't eat a bite if she sees you first. I might as well pick it up before you go in or you'll be wearing it home."

"Good idea, Hazel. She won't be hungry anyway when she hears what I've come for. Scrambled-egg yellow is *not* one of my colors." Charlene decided to run to the restroom while Hazel was clearing the room of possible missiles at her mother's disposal. Several previous outbursts had ended with objects flying out the door into the hall. Luckily, no one was hit or injured—most had learned to steer clear of that end of the corridor when Charlene came to visit.

Five minutes later, Charlene put on her happiest smile and entered the Spartan ten–by-twelve space that incarcerated one of the most infamous citizens of Kellersville. "Good morning Mamma. How are you this morning?"

Clairisse turned her head away from the door and slurred "Fine 'til you came in. I knew something was afoot when they took my breakfast without trying to gag me with a few spoonfuls first. They don't really care if I eat it or not. They just have to say they tried. The food here is not fit for pigs. I just eat to stay alive and spite you!"

"Don't do it for me, *Sweetie*." She used one of Clairisse's favorite endearments for added vinegar. "I'm sure a hunger strike would be a welcomed relief to Hazel. At least she wouldn't have to bring it in and clean up your clothes afterwards. Really Mother, you spill enough food at one meal to feed ten Chinese."

"What garbage truck did you come in on? And what the hell do you want?"

"What makes you think I want something? It's not like I never come to visit."

"Honey, I'm paralyzed and can't walk, but I can still see through you and your shit. It's too early for you to be out on business. You're dressed in a blue suit and carrying a legal envelope. I've been expecting this, but I'm not going down without a fight." Some of the slurring had disappeared because of the rush of adrenalin Clarisse always experienced when challenged.

"It's exactly what I'd do in your place. After all, as much as it must gall you, you're my daughter and for the first time in your life, you're showing some starch in your backbone. Actually, in a strange way, I'm right proud of you."

"Just makes my day to think I've done something to please you. What did I do to deserve this treat? Don't worry, I'll piss you off royally tomorrow and you'll feel better."

"Darlin', it does my heart good to see you squirm."

"Heart? What heart? They took it out years ago with your gall bladder."

"You weren't expecting me to give up without kickin' did ya?

Charlene sighed. "So, you won't sign?"

"Not just no, but hell no! You're going to have put on your cat claws and scratch for it just like I've had to do for everything I've ever gotten."

"I've already started the process. Everybody in town's just itching to see you declared *in compos mentis*. They've been standing in line for years to stab you in the back like Julius Caesar. Based on your sweetness over the years, you have so *many* friends and they all want to be on the probate panel that sends you away. See ya in court, sweetie!"

As she turned to leave, Clairisse asked "Have you heard anything from that bastard fake husband I bought for you?"

Charlene didn't hesitate as she exited the room, but Clairisse knew she had scored the first major strike.

Two

Clairisse's Last Stand

Legal proceedings to declare Clairisse incompetent were quick and relatively easy—she had pissed off the Probate Judge on several occasions and he was only too eager to retaliate. As a result, Charlene filed for control of the business as well as Clairisse's personal financial affairs. Charlene took over the family financial affairs and the day-to-day operation of the funeral business and cemetery.

The next week, Jerry came to the funeral home to talk to Charlene. Charlene was immediately told he was there, but kept him waiting for twenty minutes as a power play.

"Hey Bubba. I can't remember the last time you came here except for burying somebody. What's the occasion? You're not here to make arrangements… oh honey, why didn't you tell me? Is it you or Suzanne?" Charlene was genuinely touched and dazed. After all, he was her only brother and she had always loved and looked after him. Suzanne, on the other hand, was a different matter. Although she knew within reason that Jerry's addictive personality and Clairisse's domination were primary causes of the problem, she blamed Suzanne in part for Jerry's alcoholism—at least in her complicity.

Jerry coughed twice and began a stammering attempt to verbalize his reason for coming. "No, I'm glad to say you'll have to wait awhile to bury both of us. I've come to he…he… help run the business."

"For God's sake, Jerry. You can't be serious. Everybody in town's aware of your drinking problem. They all think you're a losing proposition as far as business dealings are concerned. Nobody's going to do business with anybody on a constant supply of hooch. You'll ruin the business."

Since neither Jerry nor Suzanne was gainfully employed, they totally depended on the family company for their sole support. Charlene, who also had relied on the family business to supplement George's church salary now assumed full control of more money than she had ever imagined and although she loved him very much, when it came to a hand out, she was not an easy mark. In fact, she became rather aloof to them; possibly a reaction to his lack of support during her takeover from Clairisse, but more probably a case of sibling rivalry coupled with a true distaste of his alcoholic lifestyle and their socially unacceptable daughter.

"Jerry, I love you very much, but we have to be realistic. I'll make you a deal. I'll pay for rehab if you'll go. When you get back, we'll run the business together. You have to take the first step to work out your problems. It's up to you. You have to really be serious. Mamma's in the loony bin and can't run your life any more. You can take control of yourself and straighten up or keep on drinking and living like a puppy. It's your choice. You let me know and I'll make the necessary arrangements."

Whether it was a realization that without drastic action it would be his destiny to live under the iron hand of another female in his family or the realization this was his last chance to change his life, he looked Charlene in the face and said, "I'll do it. What about Suzanne? Will you send her as well?"

"Yes, I guess so. But not to the same place. You need to do this by yourself."

The next day when Jerry went to visit Clairisse in the nursing home, Hazel greeted him as she was leaving Clairisse's room. "Morning, Jerry."

"Good morning, Hazel. How's the old bag today?"

"Honey," she chuckled, "she's no different. Just like the last time you came. Still sorta *testy*, if you know what I mean."

He acknowledged with a nod and grin. "I'm afraid I know all too well exactly what you mean. At least this time, I waited until *The Price is Right* was over. I surely don't want to go through *that* again!"

"Thanks. It ruined the day for all of us!"

Jerry took a deep breath and stepped into the room. "Hello, Mother."

"Well God love me! Will my good fortune never end? My prunes worked and you showed up all in the same hour. Where's that wife of yours? Have you at least spared me from her *simpy* conversation this morning?

"Mother, you know Suzanne cares as much about you as *I* do!"

"I'm well aware of that. I've always thought you married *beneath* you and lived down to her level."

"Now Mother, I'm *so surprised* to hear you feel that way. It's such a *comfort* to know I've not disappointed you all these years. You're all we've lived for these last few years."

"My money is all you've lived *off*, you mean. If it weren't for my money, you and 'Jack Daniels' wouldn't be such good friends."

"Actually, you couldn't be closer to the truth. But enough of all these compliments, I'm here to tell you some news."

"God! Don't tell me that daughter of yours is going to have another little niglet."

"No. Not that it would affect you anyway. You've banned them from the family so they never come home."

"Well, there are some benefits of being outspoken with one's opinion."

"You have such a way with *words*."

"Then, why the hell are you here. It can't be money since Charlene has snatched the purse strings right out of my hands. What can be so important that you've come here as close to sober as I've seen you in years?"

"That's the point. I'm going to Montgomery and check into a clinic to get dried out."

"Sweet Jesus! What a laugh!"

"Again, thanks for your usual confidence and support. It means so much to me to know you care."

"It doesn't make any difference if I *care* or not. It'll be a big waste of money. You'll never kick the hooch. And speaking of money, who's going to pay for it? You haven't got a pot to piss in. Those places aren't cheap!"

"I'm aware of that. Charlene said she'd pay for it and when I came back, we'd run the business together."

"God love ya! You're just one hoot after another this morning. First of all, you'll always be a drunk. I know it. You know it. And, most importantly, Charlene knows it. In fact, she's banking on it. Secondly, Charlene will *never* let you have anything to do with the company. She's on the throne and not thinking of giving up the crown."

"You're wrong, old lady! I'm coming back dried out. I won't always be a drunk, but *you* will always and forever be mentally incompetent. You have been legally certified *insane* and the only thing that's standing between you and Bryce Institute is the monthly check for your rent here. I'll be back alright, and *sober.* And I will *personally* pack your bags for the trip to Tuscaloosa. However, I hear they don't have many visitors up there, so you won't need a lot of things in the state crazy house."

"Charlene won't let me be sent to Bryce!"

"I wouldn't depend on that. If you didn't have the long-term insurance I talked you into buying, you'd be there right now."

"Get out! I'm tired of you this morning."

"Mother, I've been tired of you for years."

As he turned and walked out of the room, he heard the TV turn on. Clairisse resumed what had become the last pleasure of her miserable existence.

Three

"Ding Dong..."

Jerry turned his life around. He drove to Montgomery and admitted himself to a dry-out facility. Eighteen weeks later, he was discharged and returned to Kellersville.

Charlene lived up to her promise. She and Jerry signed a partnership agreement and they successfully ran the business together.

Jerry had been sober for seventeen months when Clairisse suffered the second major stroke, which she did not survive. When his secretary, who *always* used the intercom, knocked on the door and entered his office to announce a phone call, he immediately suspected the personal nature of the message he was about to receive. He listened carefully while the administrator of the nursing home told him his mother had suffered a fatal attack this morning. Since there was a DNR (Do Not Resuscitate) order on her chart, she passed without regaining consciousness.

"Thank you very much for all you and your staff have done for out family over the years. I'll send for her body this afternoon."

After replacing the receiver in the cradle, he walked over to the cabinet in his office, took out a bottle of scotch, poured a stiff shot in his water glass which he raised in the air, uttered the words, "Here's to your death, Mother. Now we'll all have the peace you denied us during your life!" He then poured the drink down the sink. He picked up the phone and when Charlene answered, he calmly announced, "Ding dong, the bitch is dead!"

Charlene responded "Just in time. The long-term insurance runs out next month. It's the first thing she's ever done that will please everybody. I'm sure she would've postponed her last breath if she had thought it would cause us one more problem."

Four

"The evil men do lives after them. The good is oft interred with their bones. So Let It Be With [Clairisse]."
(With Apologies to Wm. Shakespeare)

Harper certainly wasn't shocked to receive the call from Jerry, just surprised it came so soon. When he asked the funeral plans, it was mainly out of courtesy; he certainly didn't intend to fly back to Alabama for Clairisse's funeral. He was, however, very surprised when he found out how important it was for PK to go. He rapidly made plans to fly to Montgomery and rent a car. His only guess as to why PK wanted to return was closure with Nan's death. In any event, he wanted to do it for PK. He had no idea Paul would also want to go. Since it was the summer, it was a convenient time for PK.

The Mason family farm in Dawson's Ditch was equally owned by Clairisse and Harper, who had inherited his father's share. He remembered the time almost three years ago when he broached the subject of selling it to the family who was renting and farming the land. Clairisse would hear nothing of it. This would be a good time to settle this issue with Charlene and Jerry.

The harried trip to Alabama was as long as they had expected. All three wondered about the changes that had occurred in Kellersville since they left so abruptly over two years ago.

PK had just graduated from high school and was planning to attend College of the Desert and live at home. Since he graduated several months short of his eighteenth birthday, Harper and Paul were not amenable to his going off to a university boarding environment. He knew his friends would all be going off to college and although it was certainly not the primary reason he wanted to go back for the funeral, he welcomed the chance to see them again.

They checked into **the** motel at the edge of town on Wetumpka highway (a recent addition to the thriving metropolis of East Alabama). PK made several phone calls to arrange to see friends while they were in town.

When they arrived at the funeral home, the crowd was already gathered around the door to the visitation salon waiting for the family to make an official appearance to begin the hour-long session for everyone to pay respects and condolences to the survivors. Harper, PK and Paul entered the Family Meditation Room.

After the customary greetings and condolences all around, Charlene said to Harper, "Honey, I'm surprised, *pleased*, but surprised you came."

"We all needed closure on this part of our lives, PK especially because of Nan. I think he needed to come back to reassure himself she has really gone."

"How are y'all getting along?"

"We're fine. Paul finally moved in. It's easier not trying to have two places. We didn't want to push it on PK until he was ready. They get along very well. Of course, Palm Springs is more of a nurturing environment and causes almost no social problems."

"What do you hear from Hank?"

"He's still at Chapel Hill working on his doctorate. PK visited for a week during his Easter break in April. He's seeing a fellow grad student, but they're not living together yet. PK liked her a lot. She's a single parent with a ten-year-old son. I think PK sent him an email about Clairisse."

Just at that moment, the director came in to announce it was time for the family to join the friends in the reception room next door. He opened the adjoining door and they filed in to greet the usual group of Kellersville denizens who would flock to a blue jay's interment in order not to miss a single opportunity to participate in the ritual of a Southern funeralizing. Being absent at one of these gatherings was social suicide.

As they entered the room, the usual greetings, sighs, groans and lamentations began.

Charlene took her place in the official mourning wingback, about ten feet to the right of the casket. Harper's eyes were riveted on the focal point of the room, the bay window where the coffin was situated. Goose bumps ran up and down his spine—it was déjà-vu. Right in the center of an array of assorted sprays was a light-brown mahogany casket with a floral drape of yellow roses!

Harper looked at the group of old ladies hovering around the casket. There were the usual congregants: Margaret Simpson, Harriett Jensen, and the spinster emeritus, Beatrice who was saying "I heard they had to have a closed casket because the paralysis of the last stroke distorted her face so much they couldn't get her mouth straightened out."

Harriett added, "Marianne Butler said they buried her in that beautiful rose dress she wore to Charlene's last wedding. One of the pallbearers told Helen Johnson that when they moved the coffin in here, it was so light they weren't sure anyone was in it."

That remark struck Harper like a splash of cold water in the parched face of a dying man. His head snapped around and caught Charlene's attention. Evidently she had overheard the same remarks. She partially covered the sheepish grin on her face with Clairisse's black-lace handkerchief and winked at him.

Harper could smell the smoke!

www.ingramcontent.com/pod-product-compliance
Ingram Content Group UK Ltd.
Pitfield, Milton Keynes, MK11 3LW, UK
UKHW041946190726
13854UKWH00004B/1812